This is a work of fiction. Similarities to real people, places, or events are entirely coincidental.

INTERGENERATIONAL PSYCHIC MAYHEM AND OTHER WEIRD STORIES

First edition. November 15, 2025.

Copyright © 2025 Jack Opel.

ISBN: 979-8993936215

Written by Jack Opel.

I0520902

Table of Contents

Intergenerational Psychic Mayhem
and Other Weird Stories
by Jack Opel

The works in this collection of stories are fictional.

Intergenerational Psychic Mayhem

You might ask a friend, "Read any good books lately?" The two of you are out walking to get some coffee. It's late August, so you figure they've been taking some time off from work, or maybe they've just gotten back from the beach.

"I can't remember the title," your friend says, "but it's about a psychotherapist who takes on a case of intergenerational psychic mayhem. The book was about the psychotherapist and his hardest case."

"Any good?" you ask.

"Sort of what you'd expect," your friend says, as if "intergenerational psychic mayhem" is not only a clear explanation, but one you might expect.

It's the kind of stock-phrase nonsense you'd find on the cover of a paperback, or maybe a hardcover book if your friend has that kind of money. They simply write "A psychotherapist takes on a case of intergenerational psychic mayhem" along the bottom of a book cover, perhaps the word "**mayhem**" is bold and underlined. Add a catchy title and some good cover art. The Title: The Ties that Bind. The picture: An old Yankee clipper ship, its trailing ropes and pulley tackle dangled across a stormy sky, sailing over an arctic sea littered with icebergs.

You have to understand that *I'm* a psychotherapist—and a psychiatrist, a psychoanalyst— and a lot of my time is spent dealing with the transmission of psychic trauma, often intergenerational, and it frequently does verge on mayhem. Just review some literature on eating disorders.

What is psychic trauma? People fight over definitions all the time. Here's one: The physical and psychic residue of injuries caused by actions, words, and thoughts given edge and point by relationships and all their expectations. That's not perfect, but basically if we're talking about something that hurt you and you *still* feel it, really feel it, as if it's

1

happening right now, then probably fair to say, "maybe some psychic trauma there." We can't say it's elevated into mayhem, but where there's smoke, there's fire.

What exactly is this mayhem? I had this idea once for a full body "worry stone," an enormous slab of white marble that the client could roll around on as needed, shrieking if necessary. After some initial sketches, I realized that what I was thinking of was commonly called "the floor" and that many of my clients already rolled around on that, shrieking and crying, too.

So, family meetings and therapy are what I do, often if not always involving intergenerational psychic mayhem. In one of my well-rehearsed preliminaries to these sessions, so well-rehearsed that the posters I use as visuals have become frayed and even stained by spilled coffee, the "nuclear family" is displayed energetically in paper cut-out gears that actually spin on small brass tacks to show co-dependencies and other inter-psychic distortions. This concept opens up a discussion by putting into mechanical array the intricacies of otherwise individual traumas concealed in the atomized unconscious. Communicative errors, the bruises of injuries that are themselves new injuries, become the push and pull of paper teeth, grinding away at the slightest touch, often between generations, causing all sorts of psychic mayhem.

I have changed the labels on these decorative gears. Gone are the original "Father," "Mother," "Son," "Daughter," replaced by small faces that are sufficiently abstracted to remove age, gender, or other identifying features that might conjure the bogeymen of kinship, such as guilt, disappointment, and unnamable longing. I want to avoid talk about preconceived complexes or scripts or what have you. The only problem is that since the gears turn, the faces go upside down and the blankly smiling mouths become clearly frowning ones. Worse still, the faces can end up sideways, glancing at one another with sideways glances that threaten clear and productive communication between group members with their dripping innuendo and suggestion. Everyone knows, intuitively and across many cultures, that a sideways glance makes whatever a person might be saying thicker and somehow juicier, freighted and ripe with suggestions. Don't take my word for it. You can hear in someone's voice if they are glancing sideways, and I urge everyone to notice this phenomenon for themselves.

Lord knows I didn't want the job. Not "the job" of psychotherapy, just this job, this case in particular on my calendar for next week. One week in an Embassy Suites hotel in El Segundo, California, perched in a ground-floor conference room only a few miles from the airport and the West Basin sewage treatment facility. A family of *checks notes* seven, single mother, four adult children, two of these married. Three grandchildren, not in attendance. Let me guess, without reference to notes, that substance abuse disorder will be involved.

There are a lot of things about Los Angeles that people don't realize. For one, the coastline just north of the city turns west, and Pacific Palisades, Malibu, Point Dume, and all the other scenically named spots along the coast road face mostly south, almost into open ocean. Another is that the city sits in an alluvial basin, the dried remnants of a monstrously ancient riverbed. Throughout the city, planned features anticipate the return of these waters under less-than-ideal conditions called "the 100-year flood." Pan Pacific Park, with baseball diamonds, playground pavilion, and amphitheater, secretly waits as a catch-basin for storm-water run-off. The city's geological double-identity is also why some of the otherwise finest coastal real estate in the world is given over by the necessities of physical laws to process millions of gallons of sewage every day. Behold, El Segundo.

I always plan to arrive early to make arrangements, but mostly to be sure there is a round table, two love seats, several cushioned chairs with wide arm rests, and a couple of throw pillows. We've had enough adjudicative interiors, a judge's bench or the stark clinician's walls. And no clock. It's bad enough the windows open on the impoverished shrubbery of the parking lot, but a clock would be much worse for no other reason than its ceaselessness. Nothing reveals the contradictions of therapy like the measurement of time. Even the scheduling of appointments, the existence of waiting rooms, the careful "Well, that's all the time we have for today," disrupt the therapeutic process, the goal of which is complete integration with things as they are. The change of seasons or even the simple roll of the sun through the sky, or better yet the human pulse thumping in a bent wrist, is all that is required and, more importantly, not to be exceeded.

"We're having a family gathering to discuss some sensitive issues," I'll might say over the phone to an assistant hotel manager wearing an off the rack suit from JC Penney's, "and I'd like the room to be comfortable. They're coming from all over and only have a week together."

Such a limp request would get me a badly lit conference room with a board room table, high back chairs, and a giant flip chart with lots of colored markers. Why not throw in an LED display scrolling stock prices and the Dow Jones index? No thank you. If I want props, I want to rummage through a milk crate filled with sticky notes and highlighters and masking tape for them, in front of the clients. It's part of the show. I want to appear human. It doesn't matter that through the window we can see Ruby-crowned Kinglets pecking at the Burger King wrappers that have blown into the distressing foundation plantings, you know, something pathetic and engagingly metaphorical. If people trying to sort through intergenerational psychic mayhem need anything it is reminders of their humanity in its most intimate interior form. No one ever figured out the meaning of life in a criminal courtroom, a board room, a waiting room. In fact, the opposite occurs there, the meaning of not living.

For example: After I show them the gear posters, I'm careful to point out that they (the people, the clients) are not, in fact, gears. They're people, and I value each one of them. I'm not kidding.

Sure, we could do this all outside somewhere, on a beach or perhaps walking along a lonesome country road, or even around a dinner table or in the intimacy of our bedrooms just waking from sleep. But we can't. We have time to deal with, as I've mentioned, but its threat is unavoidable, and can you imagine scheduling a family meeting to encounter, as if for the first time, intergenerational psychic mayhem in our pajamas? Can there be a dress code for such an event? Meet such things head on: Round table, two love seats, comfortable chairs. Throw pillows. Dress comfortably. And, for the sake of anything holy, no clock. Sometimes you have to do something a certain way even if it's not exactly the right way.

Hmm. What else do I know "going into this," as they say? Not much, so we'll have to spend time "getting some background." There's an endless list of "icebreakers," the painful awkwardness of which provides motivation to move on to the more difficult work. The Name Game, Find Someone Who, Poker Hand, Two Truths and a Lie, This or That, Circles, Catch the Ball, What's Over Your Shoulder, If I Were a Cheese, Dog or Cat, Candles On the Cake, Vaccination, Circle Circle, Tap Tap Run, It's a Quiz, How About This, Best Birthday, You Can Call Me, Run It up the Flagpole, Solid or Liquid, Video Games Make Me Feel Happy, Let Me Introduce You, All About Me, Two Verbs and a Noun, Circles Within Circles, Salt and Vinegar, The Line Forms Here, Form a Circle.

Moving on. Ignoring training and experience, I have an innate predisposition to psychotherapy that makes "preparing" more like "this is me just walking around." It's a part of me, as is the notion of intergenerational psychic mayhem. I'm a catalyst, akin to platinum, thirty times rarer than gold and found most frequently in alluvial river sands. Of course I'm prepared for dealing with things psychotherapeutic. You know about those posters, right, the gear ones with faces? I've studied this stuff, gone to schools and universities, attended trainings and seminars, worked under the supervision of other psychotherapists—in hospitals, clinics, emergency rooms, pediatric psychiatry wards, out-patient drug treatment facilities, you name it—but I have cast a far wider net because I am, in a way, a wide net. I've studied cross-cultural anthropology; demonology and the medieval Catholic church; the political economy of Laos; teaching practice in the post-Katrina school system of New Orleans; Jewish identity and the founding of Israel; Abyssinian numismatics; Jackson Pollock's early work; the influence of Sumerian myth on the deepest structures of meaning in what would become "The West."

Breadth, depth, any numerable dimensions of study. Unlike other professions, if you want to list psychotherapy among professions, specialized training isn't something divorced from everything else; it's ontological. Lawyers learn to "think like a lawyer" and doctors get to "play doctor" and politicians "run for office" and "stand for their constituents." For me (and by "me" I mean any psychotherapist, even those without formal medical training), "Homo sum: humani nihil a me allenum puto" is more than well-worn truism, but rather a grim imprecation weighing more heavily with each new day. We go willingly, instinctively perhaps, into the underworld on a quest from which we can never return, to dwell forever with the shades.

This is a lifelong interest. As a child, the only child of older parents, I participated in family therapy that my mother insisted upon to avoid a divorce. My father was a reclusive man, a war veteran whose quiet demeanor never broke, even though he drank heavily and played golf with comically out-sized men who worked in advertising, insurance, or "sales," nebulous employments that left them plenty of time, both for golf and heavy drinking. It wasn't mere neglect that bothered my mother, I believe, but my father's certain inert contentedness with banality. I remember the "last straw," as she put it, a summer cocktail party that went late into the night, the men all wearing their tackiest golfing pants—patterns with roses, smiley faces, or large polka dots best suited for clowns; tartans, zig-zags, argyles, paisleys; every shade of lime, lemon, and orange— slapping each other on the back while swilling booze, the women having gone to the kitchen to sip highballs, smoke, and quietly complain to one another.

As the party wound down around midnight, Mr. Smith (not his real name) and his wife drove off. Halfway down the driveway, he drunkenly swerved onto the lawn, through several low hedges, and then out over a large, flat outcropping of stone. Sparks flew as the enormous 1973 Chevrolet Impala leaped over the edge, some five feet off the ground, then caromed off the pavement below and sped away, leaving most of the car's exhaust system behind for the scavengers.

"That's the last straw," my mother said, putting a cigarette out in a highball glass, and the next week we went to see Dr. Denaif as a family. Other than these circumstances, all I remember distinctly was playing Rock'em, Sock'em Robots for the first time. But my parents did not divorce, and Dr. Denaif seemed like the most reasonable adult man I had ever met. That stays with an impressionable boy of eight, let me tell you.

Nonetheless, I worked as a mortician in my twenties. I was only fourteen when my parents died, and the relatives to whom I was entrusted did little to encourage anything but narrowly vocational education, and as there was a very small private not-for-profit two year school in the area devoted exclusively to mortuary science and funeral service management, fate cast a blow that had me spending ten years in the craft.

On the eve of my thirtieth birthday, however, I attended my first wedding as an adult. Two things. First, wedding events are strikingly similar to funerals, and I found myself at the reception, chatting with the planner about catering. Second, she mentioned, casually, that she was about to quit and go to medical school, specifically one that waived tuition. I had no idea such a thing existed, yet she rattled off several names: Uniformed Services University, Kaiser Permanente Bernard J. Tyson School of Medicine, NYU Grossman School of Medicine. All free.

At the time I lived in a large apartment above the funeral home with a roommate whose sole ambition was to marry the owner's daughter, and I admit that she was a lovely woman with many appealing characteristics aside from her parentage. But when she announced her engagement (to the roommate, not to me) I couldn't shake the idea of medical school. For free.

I had been reading extensively in my spare time, mostly in an undisciplined way along lines of interest that would sharpen later in life, but for a time I committed to night classes at the community college and gained prerequisites, a Bachelor's degree, and intensive preparation for the MCAT examination. Three years I thus toiled, but at thirty-three I was off to California and medical school.

I might sound like a broken record, but medical school and the study of mortuary science bear a strong resemblance; more importantly, psychiatry, and even more so psychotherapy, are practically the same thing.

After graduation, I took six weeks off before my residency as a psychiatrist. I was exhausted and knew it, but my twisting fate offered good fortune in a friend whose family owned a ranch outside Billings, Montana, to which we retreated for over a month. All of it was good for me, the open space, horses, hearty food. What struck me at the core was, you guessed it, the profound intergenerational psychic mayhem. My friend had nine siblings, five brothers and four sisters, all married with small children. They all lived and worked on or near the ranch. His parents and both sets of grandparents likewise, having combined their neighboring operations. What I witnessed go on beneath that folksy veneer would shame the Borgias.

What I carried away from Montana stayed with me ever after; I felt that intergenerational psychic mayhem had manifested to me, like a prophetic vision before a saint kneeling in a grotto. It had marked me its witness and prophet, and a concomitant fervor descended. Wherever I went, whenever I encountered intergenerational psychic mayhem, skittering like downed power lines in the rain, I felt a strange protection. I could just walk up, touch the wires and, lo, I would not die. The rest, as they say, is history.

But it goes deeper than that. Over the years, I've changed. Those first revelations in Montana transformed my nature, but the years since have wrought something magnificent, a lapidary perfection of sorts. It seems crazy to say, but I am bound up with intergenerational psychic mayhem in a molecular way, tied to it, woven into it.

Imagine a family. Now imagine a "perfect family." I'm not going to flesh that out any more than that, a "perfect family." Are they on a vacation that each one of them is enjoying? Have they spent an afternoon together, hiking on woodland trails or through fields of wildflowers dancing under the fresh sky of June, only to come across a doe with her fawn, just standing there in the path and not even running away? Did mom and dad make everyone's favorite dinner, russet-brown fried chicken and mashed potatoes, working together playfully in the kitchen? Followed, perhaps, by some board games or a collective viewing of that new movie, a comedy, which happily is refreshingly light on vulgar language? That kind of perfect family. And, no, they don't have to be Mormon.

If you put a frame around this perfect family, a tasteful frame that you would be happy to have on the mantel piece in your living room or maybe even the dresser in your bedroom, inside that frame I do not exist, cannot exist, never existed. I may have existed as some other family's psychotherapist, maybe some friends of the perfect family, but that's a different me.

Now, if we change this thought experiment completely, make imperfect our perfect family, laden them with pain and guilt, but especially the kind of pain and guilt caused by words and thoughts given edge and point by relationships and all their expectations, I still don't exist yet. Perhaps you look at this new picture, a picture of this imperfect family that has replaced the other one, and incant "intergenerational psychic mayhem" with the slightest breath, but that, while necessary, is insufficient. I still don't exist.

It could happen this way to our now imperfect family. Mother takes the kids to the bookstore. Father is in a bad mood: Work is hard or something. He's bored, but underneath all that there is something gnawing. Why is his son struggling in school? His daughter not popular? His wife no longer the "woman he married?" He drinks too much.

Mother can be angry, too, which is just another way of saying she's sad. She thinks "I've turned into my mother." She drinks, too. Then there's Brad, her old boyfriend. He's divorced now and been calling "just to catch up." Storm clouds on the horizon.

The children are confused, which is also to say they are sad, but that could be in the way children are sad because childhood is sad.

These parts of the story would be quite extensive, just like those storm clouds blowing on mom, presenting infinite fractal depth. Every unhappy family, etc. I have spared you more specific details out of professional concern for your safety. Trust me. I know what I'm talking about.

Back to the bookstore. Mother, turning down an aisle at random—the children know exactly where to go in a bookstore and have already gone there—turning down this random aisle, mother sips her soy-latte and finds herself staring at a shelf of self-help books. And there it is: The Ties that Bind, the cover photograph so vivid she can feel the icy wind that snaps those well-worn sails. Here, she reads across the bottom, "A psychotherapist takes on a case of intergenerational psychic **mayhem.**" And thus, I have begun to materialize. Inside the frame on the mantel piece or the one on the bedroom dresser, particles of silver nitrate reassemble to usher my umbral presence into this imperfect family's world, and with it so much more we can only hope. I will be with them soon. It will be a better world, and those who dwell within it will one day emerge into the warm light of day, even if we say so with sideways glance.

Old Quaker Graveyard

O ld Route 120 was a worn-out macadam road that ran through the center of town, over a crumbling bridge that crossed the run-down train tracks, and then up into the small hills to the south. After several miles, it passed a summer camp for disabled children that sat empty for all but July and August. Across the street was an old Quaker graveyard with a wall around it made of piled granite, filled with worn and faded headstones that tilted unevenly like ocean swells in the winter. When the camp was in session, the counselors took the campers there on hot days to eat lunch under the large trees that lined the back. One time they threw a birthday party there, decorating the lower tree branches with pastel crepe streamers. A magician performed his magic tricks, wearing a tuxedo and using an actual top hat. They also square danced and played pin the tail on the donkey. At the end, they all decorated their own cupcakes with frosting and different kinds of sprinkles.

Near the old Quaker graveyard was a house. It was also across the street from the summer camp for disabled children, which sprawled along for almost a mile. This house was built in 1740, a timber frame building with white clapboards and a balcony along the second floor fronting the road, supported by square posts. The shingles on the low-sloped roof were very old, warped and tinged with green moss. A red-haired boy lived there with his mother, who was an invalid of sorts. He often walked to town by himself to play with the other children, since no one else lived out there. Everyone knew about this little family and that the mother couldn't drive, so anyone driving on Old Route 120 would usually stop to give the red-haired boy a ride into town or back home. He was a sweet and friendly child who would always tell the story of how George Washington had slept in his house, after the Battle of White Plains.

One time a driver asked the red-haired boy if he had ever seen George Washington's ghost.

"No," said the boy. "The ghosts are in the graveyard."

Since the summer camp for disabled children was empty for all but two months of the year, the children from town sometimes explored there, which delighted the red-haired boy. He knew all the secrets of the summer camp, and when the other children came to explore, he would lead them from place to place. A road curved through the camp in a big semi-circle, starting at the gate across from the old Quaker graveyard. Above the gate a sign hung on chains with the camp's name carved in large letters on a wood plank, "Pilgrim Summer Camp." The gate was never locked, and usually it was pushed back and held open with one of the large granite rocks from the wall around the graveyard.

The first thing on the road inside the camp was the lodge. It had been an old Quaker meeting house, built from logs cut down when they cleared the land for the old Quaker graveyard, back in 1740. There had been improvements to it when the land became a summer camp for disabled children, so that it resembled a Wild West themed frontier outpost tourist attraction, with a covered porch, ramp for wheelchair access, large windows, and glass double-doors. The children would press their faces against the doors and peer in at the rows of Formica-topped tables and the stainless-steel cafeteria counter, and the red-haired boy would point out that they even had a soft ice cream dispenser, over there in the corner. He had also seen the disabled campers at the birthday party in the graveyard, and the magician, and the cupcakes they were decorating. The children thought about how fun it would be to be a camper at the summer camp for disabled children.

As the camp's semi-circle road wound through tall pine trees, on either side were prefabricated buildings with more tidy signs with letters carved on wood planks. "Arts & Crafts" read one, "Photography" another, "Infirmary" yet another, each at the start of a well-maintained gravel path leading up to the building. The children seemed to know, instinctively, that these were from the 1970s. There was an empty swimming pool, a soccer field, and an archery range, although the targets were all put away in a storage shed at the back.

The bunkhouses came next, five long buildings with plywood shutters, arranged in a circle like spokes of a wheel. In the middle was a fire pit ring made of stones. The only other building was another shed, and if you pulled the door open a crack you could see two lawnmowers and a can of gas.

The semi-circular road ended back at old Route 120 across from the red-haired boy's house. Just before the exit, a small stream ran into a culvert and underneath the road. There was a sluice of sorts in the culvert, and in October, after the camp was all closed up, someone, the red-haired boy didn't know who, came and closed it. The marshy land between the semi-circle camp road and old Route 120 would flood, and when it froze, people would drive out from town and ice skate. It was a nice thing the camp did for everybody.

"Do you guys know about Baby Ruby?" said the red-haired boy.

No one did.

"This happened a long time ago, but my mother told me about Baby Ruby. She doesn't like me coming over here, but she said it was okay as long as I stay out of there," the red-haired boy said, pointing at the culvert.

"A long time ago, when the camp was first opened, there was an older camper who was kind of slow but really sweet. His name was Baby Ruby, maybe some kind of nickname, I guess. Anyway, they called him Baby Ruby, or maybe he called himself that. I don't know.

"He liked to play hide and seek, and he was really good at it. Every night they would play games after dinner, like kick ball and capture the flag, but Baby Ruby liked to play hide and seek the most. All the campers would hide all over the camp, and then the counselors would find them. And they played hide and seek the way that once you're found, you help find, so after a while there are a lot more seekers than campers hiding.

"One night they were playing and the game went on and on. It seemed like all the campers were found, so they checked, but Baby Ruby was still hiding. He was the only one. So, all the campers and all the counselors go around shouting for Baby Ruby to come out, he's won the game. That happened a lot because Baby Ruby was really good at hiding.

"It gets dark and they still haven't found Baby Ruby. The counselors start to get worried. Some of them put the campers to bed, and the others keep looking for Baby Ruby. They called the police, and they came and everyone kept searching all night. No luck. The next day, they kept searching, looking over in the graveyard, over on Hardscrabble Road. Everywhere.

"Then, after lunch a counselor noticed," the red-haired boy said, pointing to the marshy land inside the semi-circle. "It was starting to flood, just like in winter."

The children looked horrified.

"Baby Ruby was stuck in there," the red-haired boy said, pointing at the culvert again.

"Was he dead?" one of the children asked.

"Yup," the red-haired boy said, nodding solemnly. "They put that grate on there, but you can still get in on the other side. I've never done it. I promised my mother. It kinda scares me, too."

The children agreed. It kind of scared them as well.

Life went on for the red-haired boy. His mother got sicker, and she went to live in a nursing home across from the drug store in town. He went to live with his aunt near town. The nursing home was just an old house that had been turned into a nursing home. It had a big porch and some of the residents were "vets," and others were just sick or old like his mother. When it was warm, the vets would sit on the porch all day smoking. His aunt's house was a "split level ranch house," but the red-haired boy thought it looked like a television house, something the Brady Bunch would live in. His aunt wasn't married and didn't have children, and it was a big house. She was a realtor.

She lived on Hardscrabble Road, which wasn't exactly a dirt road, but it wasn't really paved either. If you drove into town on Old Route 120, you turned right on Hardscrabble Road about halfway there and then drove a mile or two to his aunt's house, so it was closer to town, but still pretty far. The good news was that there was a path in the backyard that cut through the woods and straight into town near the train station, and since it was a straight shot it only took about ten minutes to get there.

The path went through a forest with enormous trees that the red-haired boy liked to climb. The ground was covered with pine needles so thick it was like a carpet, and there were big piles of them that formed wells around the bases of some of the trees. These filled with water sometimes, and because of the pine needles the water turned a golden color.

One day the red-haired boy was walking to town to see his mother. He was carrying a tub of cheddar cheese popcorn his aunt had gotten as a present from a title insurance company, and he was supposed to bring it to the nursing home for the vets because "it's important to think about the less fortunate." He came over a rise, and there, in the water around one of the trees, two children were standing. The water came up to their chests.

They had seen a drowned rabbit floating in the water and decided to fish it out but fell in instead. When they tried to climb out the pine needles just gave way and they slipped back in. The red-haired boy dragged a big branch over to the water and put it in so they could climb out. It was a cold day, and the children had been in the water for a long time. They were shivering and scared, so the red-haired boy decided they should eat some of the cheddar cheese popcorn for energy before they headed home.

Later, when he handed the opened tub of cheddar cheese popcorn to the vets sitting on the porch, he apologized for it being open and explained about the two children stuck in the water.

"You ever hear about Baby Ruby?" said one of the vets, a tall man everyone called "Wiggles."

Of course, the red-haired boy had heard about Baby Ruby, but his mother said it was rude to be a know-it-all, so he said no.

Wiggles told the story of Baby Ruby, but it changed about halfway through.

"And they were playing hide'n seek, just like always, but Baby Ruby got found right at the beginning. He didn't like that, poor boy, and ran off crying, but it was dark already and they couldn't catch him. Got stopped up under the road where the creek goes through. Didn't find him for two days, when the skating pond flooded."

The red-haired boy sat quietly, letting that sink in. It made things different somehow, but he couldn't say why.

"You be careful out there," Wiggles said.

His mother wasn't doing too well that day. Some days she would sit up and ask him about school. He was in eighth grade now, playing soccer, and even had a first kiss with Jeannie Mazzella after a sock hop, so there was plenty to talk about (or not) and she seemed to like that he was getting older. On bad days, she would smile at him, then doze off. She had an oxygen mask and the machine it was connected to made pumping and hissing noises. She would just lie there with a blank look on her face. They said she had "idiopathic pulmonary fibrosis," which meant that her lungs were weak, and no one really knew why.

As he was getting ready to leave, she woke up.

"It's so nice to see you," she whispered. "You're a good boy."

"Nice to see you, mom," he said. "I'm going to head back. Dinner is at six tonight."

"Can you do me a favor?" she said.

He nodded tightly.

"Can you go back to the house and get my blue house coat? It's hanging on the door of my closet. No rush. I think I would like to get in a wheelchair and sit by the window."

He promised he would and kissed her on the forehead.

After soccer practice the next day, the boy walked to the house. It was a long way, but his aunt had a showing, and his bicycle had a flat tire. He went to his mother's room to fetch the blue housecoat, grabbing it off the hook in her closet. As he turned to leave, he looked out the window into the old Quaker graveyard. For a second he thought he saw something, a person maybe, standing behind one of the big trees in the back. He stared for a minute, and again he saw someone, just behind the tree, sticking their head out, then pulling back, as if they were hiding there and spying on the house. A hand reached around the side of the tree then was snatched back.

Clutching the blue house coat, the boy ran out into the old Quaker graveyard to see who it was, darting from one tree to the next, but no one was there.

The red-haired boy's mother died in late June. They told him that she just stopped breathing, but the truth was that she threw up some blood, struggled to breath for a few minutes, and then her heart stopped. All the vets and his aunt came to the funeral, which was held at St. John's, across from the grocery store.

There was the old house to deal with. As a realtor, the aunt knew how to stage an historic property for sale, but since it was so far out of town and right next to the old Quaker graveyard, it was going to be a challenge. Before she listed the house for sale, she wanted her nephew to pack up anything he wanted to keep. School had just let out a few weeks ago, and the red-haired boy was cutting lawns for a landscaper named Pete, who had known his mother and felt sorry for him. Pete gave him a few days off and paid him anyway.

"You take some time and sort things out," Pete said.

The aunt offered to drop the boy off at the house; it was a Sunday, and she had several showings, but he could spend as much time as he needed going through the house. He said no, that he wanted to walk.

He got to the house around noon, and the air was still and warm. The house seemed dark, the windows dirty, and the small driveway was littered with leaves and pine needles. As he stood in the small front hallway, it wasn't clear to him exactly what he should be going through in the house. All his clothes were at his aunt's, as well as all the things from his room, like the airplane models and posters. There were books in the cramped living room: A set of encyclopedias, some romance novels his mother used to read, and old photo albums filled with pictures of people he didn't know. The basement had old paint cans and a dehumidifier. There was nothing of interest in the kitchen. Back in the front hall, poking out of the umbrella stand by the coat rack, was an old cane that his grandfather had used.

His mother's room was last. The top of the dresser was cramped with half-empty cosmetic jars, its drawers filled with faded and indefinable clothing. The mattress was bare, and the nightstand held only an opened package of gum and a few pencils.

As the red-haired boy turned to leave, he looked out the window again, remembering the person hiding behind the tree. He waited a minute or two, hoping to see the head again, with its tousled brown hair, or the furtive hand clutching the bark of the tree. Nothing happened. As he turned to leave there *was* something, further away, up the slope where the graveyard touched the forest. A man in black wearing a hat was turning in a circle waving his arms. The red-haired boy watched, unsure who he could be or what he was doing. And then he saw the streamers, further on, strung across the low branches of the trees.

Breaking away, he ran downstairs and out the side door into the graveyard. He went up the slope toward the turning man, and he could see he was wearing a cape that flared as he turned. Under the streamers were children sitting in a circle eating cupcakes. There was the faintest music, too, like a carousel. Other children were laughing, running between the headstones. Bewildered, he stopped and looked around, confused by what was going on. Had the summer camp for disabled children opened early this year? Then he saw it again, peering out at him from behind a tree. A head. It was a brown-haired boy about his age. The red-haired boy walked toward him.

"Hey," the red-haired boy said. "Hey, who are you?"

Before he'd taken more than a few steps, the brown-haired boy pushed away from the tree, running awkwardly down the hill towards Old Route 120.

"Hey!" the red-haired boy yelled and ran after him. "Wait up."

They ran across the old Quaker graveyard, past the old house, to the camp entrance near the culvert. The brown-haired boy was fast, but not too fast, and he kept looking back at the red-haired boy, laughing. No, it was more like giggling. His voice was almost girlish.

The brown-haired boy ran across the road and along the shoulder, turning into the summer camp for disabled children. The red-haired boy followed him, almost falling as he slipped on the sand in the rain gutter. He caught sight of the other boy just as he leaped off the camp road where it crossed the stream. Stepping to the edge of the road and peering over, he saw the other boy's legs as they disappeared at the open end of the culvert.

"You better get out of there," said the red-haired boy. "It's dangerous."

The brown-haired boy's muffled laughter echoed from the culvert.

"No, seriously," said the red-haired boy, bending over the opening and peering up. "A boy died in there, a long time ago."

The culvert was dark and still. He wondered how far up the other boy had crawled.

"Take my hand," the red-haired boy said, climbing in.

The water running in the culvert was cold and his pants got wet, but he pressed on either side and crawled like a spider, moving slowly in the dark. And then the hands grabbed him.

The next day the pond began to flood.

New Fort Lauderdale

The design and construction of New Fort Lauderdale embodies the spirit of practical innovation suggested by New Urbanism. It is a city built on and for human experience.

By day, the city is a line of mammoth cereal box hotels on a spit of land running north south off the coast of Florida. There's a crescent bay to the west, between it and the mainland. To the east yawns the indifferent Atlantic. The city is purpose built. The hatch work of streets around the hotels is jammed with two-story buildings hardened by design to withstand the surge of spring break crowds. The beaches are white sand, but artificial, like the rest of the city; underneath is a concrete shelf that transmits a brutal solidity to the surface, and running on the beach is a jarring experience. Each stride is like an elevator ride that comes to an abrupt halt.

Every city block is 310 feet long and 400 feet wide. The streets are all two way, and every fourth cross-street is a pedestrian mall filled with bad public art built on a monumental scale. These include fountains, gargantuan metal cubes, towering curved walls of unspecified stone, and at the exact center of the island a corkscrew of steel girders that rises 100 feet, all in a coordinated design that directs foot traffic in circular patterns and chokes off crowd movement in the event of a large scale riot or any panicked rush during natural or other disasters. All utilities are buried.

There are three palm trees at every corner, with another cluster mid-block. Cross walks are 'all way,' throwing up red lights to traffic in every direction and unleashing pedestrians for 25 seconds. The traffic lights are timed so that a car driving north to south on any street at 30 miles per hour, such as a police cruiser, will hit all green lights. At night, the quaintly faux-antique colonial lamp posts that light the streets, copied from an 1880 Currier & Ives print of 'A Boston Harbor Scene,' flicker to life fifteen minutes before sunset and snap off fifteen minutes before sunrise. Together with the ambient light from street level businesses and the twenty-five barbarous hotels surrounded by associated development, the city is continuously visible from space as a geometric regularity punctuated by bands of street in a coded uniformity.

Access to the city from the mainland occurs at three points: the north and south bridges, and a flat causeway across the bay that connects at the midpoint. The bridges are identical in construction, following the model of Cape Cod's Sagamore bridge. These allow cruise ship access along dredged channels into the north and south sections of the bay, which are also dredged. The causeway has pedestrian access from the city to a halfway point, where a three-acre elevated park is built to cover the roadway. Both the bridges can be raised, and the causeway has a retractable section near the mainland, so the city can cut off land access as needed.

Spring break is a roughly two-week period in March and April, depending on the calendaring of Easter, during which college students descend on the city. Since the construction of New Fort Lauderdale, there has been a spontaneous expansion to three weeks, with calls for an entire month. During spring break, the population of the city swells to roughly 50,000, excluding the substantial number of day visitors. The rest of the year, visitors are almost entirely from cruise ship lines out of the Caribbean that utilize the south bay. Off-season visitors tend simply to wander the mostly empty streets, like explorers in an abandoned city.

Most students arrive on buses over the north bridge, unloading at a regional bus terminal that doubles as a welcome center and hub for hotel shuttles. Some buses are overnighters, with reclining chairs, food service, and entertainment, including live music, stand-up comedians, and dancers. The other buses come from the airport, nominally serving the entire region, but with more than 70% of service focused on the spring break season. Cruise ships from Boston, New York, Cape

Liberty, Baltimore, Norfolk, and Charleston stream into the north bay and unload at a terminal on the elevated causeway park. Train service was scuttled in the early design phase.

With the mixture of travel modes, there is no set rhythm to crowd flow; on any given day during spring break, thousands may be arriving and leaving, giving entry points and all surface traffic and the crowds themselves a strangely uneven and fluid quality. New arrivals tend to ring the edges, while the already "broke" visitors crowd the center. Bright-eyed buoyancy and freshness mixes with exhaustion. This is not Las Vegas, however, with cheerful hordes flowing in and distraught and disappointed stragglers departing. Las Vegas, the great dystopian contradiction of urban America, is a manifest reality of something that doesn't exist, an architecturally ahistorical perfection of America's Manifest Destiny iconography. Somehow it claims the pinnacle of luxurious excess, while tourists in flip flops stumble through the streets drinking purple margaritas from plastic tubes. It promises instant wealth but offers odds that favor the house. It suspends the promise of the American dream against the truth of wealth disparity and for-profit health care. It takes either/or and rewrites it as a lie, both/and, loudly and in bright colors. Enjoy your plastic cup of silver dollars.

New Fort Lauderdale succeeds where Las Vegas fails. The city's superbly thorough and exact concept blends contradictions into a seamlessly gelatinous exchange that leads to contained excess. The crowds do not flow, they circulate, from bus or cruise ship terminal to hotel lobby welcome parties to all night volleyball and spotlight beach dance offs, then back again. The movement is tidal, both regular and marked by predictable peaks and lows.

It starts with arrival: Welcome drinks are handed out right off the bus. Hotel registration is accelerated and prearranged. Guests have room keys in hand within five minutes, guaranteed, and banks of dedicated high-speed elevators await. An activity schedule is broadcast on a jumbotron in every hotel lobby, and the pedestrian malls have constant announcements. There is a small army of facilitators, much like those at Japanese cultural festivals, who blend in and provide assistance, such as taking photographs for groups or providing directions and condoms.

Each hotel follows the same pattern and yet deploys distinctive themes and content in the specifics. One may be a tropical adventure, another a frontier experience, yet another a French village or trianon. Spring breakers can visit dance floors, rooftop bars, tiki huts, swimming pools, sandy beaches, even bowling alleys and video game arcades. There are para-sailing excursions, sailboats, kayaks, water skiing, even fishing, both from the causeway and fishing boats. Against the perfection of its measurable shapes, the line of its curbs and the contours of its foundational planning, the city manifests as a profusion of diversity that is, in essence, all the same thing. Its terrible beauty lacks contradiction, pursuing instead an intense unified profusion. It is everything that is Cancun, Acapulco, Daytona Beach, Reno, Disneyland, anyplace and no place.

After arrival, more drinks in the lobby and a brief orientation. This includes detailed information about the geography, services, and personnel on the island. Surprisingly, these are well-attended, and the audience has consistently responded favorably on customer surveys, noting that "It was good to know what I was getting into," and "The police officer was cute!" and "It would help to know the emergency code." The point is the audience pays attention.

And remember that the entire project, mission, and purpose of this place is to host spring break. And what is spring break? Prosaically, it is a brief hiatus during spring semester, usually timed around the Easter holiday, for college students to travel and relax. That's what the brochures will tell you, slinging their AI copy to pitch a two-bedroom rental in the original Fort Lauderdale, circa 2024. New Fort Lauderdale, as you have seen, extends. Break here is less "take a break" than "break from reality." But this suggests a new clarity, liberation, and extension of the self. We mean "break" as in achieve lift off, break from orbit, 'slip the surly bonds of earth and touch the face of God.' Spring break and beyond spring break. The place itself can only set the scene, so to speak. It works catalytically. The place does not change, yet those who occupy it do.

You will notice the women first, their indistinct youth, clearly adult but clinging to juvenile proclivities: Long necks and arms, revealing but expensive clothing, winsome manners that still harbor suggestive possibilities, the faint allure of sexual availability mixed with the wholesome. The usual tendency to travel in groups persists, but the groups combine, decompose, and recombine depending on movement and activity. For example, several hundred women might encounter one of the many street vendors selling alcoholic beverages. For efficiency, these vendors specialize in one product. If the beverage is, say, pina colada, the simple fact of taste will break off part of the group. Or, if the group is on a pedestrian street, one of the large sculptures will narrow the passage and divide the group or simply deflect part of the crowd in another direction when they run into it.

The men share many of these qualities, inflected with masculine vigor. There is an unavoidable incidence of zip-on personality, backwards hats, bad tattoos, and fraternity insignia. Careful attention reveals more, a striving energy that leads to spontaneous wrestling matches, foot races, football games, the singing of songs. Hotels sponsor teams to compete in games, complete with uniforms, anthems, and cheerleaders. There are several small stadiums with corporate sponsorship aimed at a youth market.

Where the women's groups are usually focused on a goal, such as going to *that* store, beach, or restaurant, the men's groups are more spontaneous, forming and breaking apart seemingly at random. In large groups, they may briefly resonate with camps of Greek warriors before the walls of fabled Iliad illumined by firelight, although these moments pass quickly back into smaller groups cheering each other on at beer chugging, arm wrestling, etc.

The crowd's expressive energy adumbrates the potential range of identities that manifests in the thronging spring break crowd of New Fort Lauderdale. Stereotypical behavior disintegrates and, taking the spring break as a complete cycle, the energy of "breaking" builds in waves. Individuals, considered as composites or molecules that combine different attributes, begin to break into small pieces that are free to exchange elements and recombine, in much the same way stars generate long-chain carbon molecules in the interstellar medium. Clothing is exchanged freely. Men in brassieres, women in jock straps, the kind of gross cross-dressing seen in the predictable skits at a spring folly show. But the wrangling mob of New Fort Lauderdale sheds the normal. More precisely, it elevates the normal to a universal. Elevated in this way it releases everything else. Drag shows are staged up and down Center Street, the main pedestrian mall. As the days wear on, these become spontaneous and blend into the entire experience. Backwards hats and feather boas. Daisy dukes and big wallets. Boots and bathing suits. Spring break participants exchange articles of clothing, and with them behaviors. There are groups of the most advanced spring breakers where there is no longer any clear notion of conventional gender.

Semi-nudity, always somewhat tolerated, gives way to dancing naked beneath that steel girder corkscrew, climbing on it, racing in a climb to the top. Crowing from its top at the moon. All this is summed up by the philosopher Elise Manon when she writes that "New Fort Lauderdale is the perfection of America as crucible, heating diverse elements for recombination and a renewed expression."

Where Las Vegas marks the divine apogee of middle-class abhorrence, New Fort Lauderdale is its fulmination, a brilliant, controlled detonation timed to the rites of spring. This is all by design, a contrived spontaneity sustained by the physical environment but also conjured by its professional acolytes. We have mentioned the facilitators, but these are not to be confused with the aspiring travel agents or fashion models one sees at car shows off the Las Vegas strip. They have none of the calculated restraint of casino employees or the psychology of sex workers.

Facilitators are carefully recruited using psychological profiling similar to that developed to track serial killers. Most are highly reluctant at first, and so initial compensation is highly competitive. Returning facilitators are actually paid less. Their role is a complicated one, part surrogate, part instigator, modeling behavior and attitudes but always able to pull back. For, while facilitators help the spring break crowd arrive, unpack, and enter the throngs, the more challenging task is to extract participants and send them back.

Extraction is one of the functions enhanced by the constant recording conducted on New Fort Lauderdale. Surveillance is complete, from ground level cameras to a fleet of drones. A satellite is used to gauge overall patterns in the crowd. Facilitators review footage looking for signs that the spring break experience has exhausted its potential. Facial recognition software identifies expressions of joy and peace, and facilitators in the area are dispatched to conduct "candidate interviews." A candidate may report a sense of warmth in their heart, heightened intuition, feelings of profound love for others, and optimism about their life struggles. Candidates also claim they "see things clearly now" and "it's going to be all right." Accounts of spontaneous healing of physical injuries are common, as are persistent physical sensations, such as goosebumps or tingling. Escorted by facilitators back to their hotels, candidates will sometimes fall into deeply meditative or prayer-like states, sitting in hotel lobbies sipping ginger ale for hours. They are then assisted in packing, loaded on the hotel shuttles, taken to the welcome center, and leave New Fort Lauderdale.

The recordings have other uses. Different editions are created for different audiences. Short, comical clips circulate on youth oriented social media. Longer compendiums are consumed by middle market cable channels. These are fashioned to present a narrative of self-discovery, personal liberation, and camaraderie. Even longer versions are used by sociologists, psychologists, and political consultants, and include as much conversation among spring breakers as possible, especially at meals and while preparing for athletic competitions or the many amateur fashion shows. The complete record is provided to the NSA, CIA, FBI, and Department of Agricultural.

By late April, life in New Fort Lauderdale dies down to an off-season lull that is practically a hibernation. As mentioned, cruise ships visit, but the city is regarded as an oddity, except for the fishing opportunities. Maintenance crews work through a careful process of cleaning and protection for the hurricane season. From October to late February the city is left with a skeleton crew. Even though the vast majority of employment is seasonal, it is both sufficiently taxing and well compensated that almost the entire work force retreats elsewhere to recover. Then, as spring approaches they return, refurbishment begins, and New Fort Lauderdale is restored. Staff are briefed on trends in social media, the latest wave of reality television, sports, fashion. There is a debriefing presentation based on the off-season analysis of last year's recordings, highlighting both successes and failures. And then, sometime in March or April, depending on the calendaring of Easter, the first bus arrives. For reasons of tradition, this is at night. The city and all the buildings remain unlit as the bus crosses the north bridge and travels through the darkened streets to the welcome center. The first spring breakers exit the bus and pass through the circular doors to street level, where the staff assemble on either side in welcome. Together, they look up and behold the stars. The city lights come on at once, the stars disappearing in the flood of pollution. Spring break begins again.

Burning House

I'm not saying I would burn down my house, or anyone's house, but in some secret core or clavicle I don't think it would be a bad thing. I'd regret losing photographs, artwork (especially the work by Beers and Kahn), and I would certainly protect people and pets in every way possible, but the rest of it? Maybe I'd toss the art through a window or shuttle out the table on which I've stacked the photo albums and boxes of stray photos.

I don't savor the prospect of losing everything. My computer files are all backed up in cloud storage (I have electronic media backups, too, but they're duplicative), so no worry there. IRS audit? Go right ahead, so sorry, everything was destroyed in a house fire. I no longer wear suits much, and I'm going to give away all but my funeral suit, the blue one my wife likes, the Edwardian formal dress, and the Prince of Wales. The rest of my clothing is fungible, except perhaps a few of the slogan T-Shirts, notably the Ernest Scared Stupid (which has coffee stains) and Vampire Circus. All my ties are mediocre. Dishes are dishes, so who cares? Books are easily replaced, and the ones I like and reread are almost all worn out.

Far from destroying stuff that I (except as noted) don't really care about, a fire would let me re-equip with the bare minimum in a fresh space that I or my heirs could sell easily and enjoy in much the same way, although the barn I currently live in has its own completely distinct aura and communal elements. I'd miss those.

Imagine waking up by the side of the road somewhere, enough money in your wallet to do what you want, but with little else. Everything gone but still the power to command a future. It doesn't bother me. The idea of mementos and keepsakes has no appeal, and the things I own are valuable only if they are useful. How many times have you visited someone, and you notice something on a shelf, say a spent artillery shell, and ask "What's the story with that thing?"

You might get a story about coastal defense during the war, something about grandpa being in the Coast Guard transporting German prisoners of war from Manhattan to Maine by sea. The spent shell isn't necessary for the story. Sure, it serves as a reminder, but there's a danger in relying on props rather than memory.

My sister-in-law's sister's son married into a family that incessantly videotaped their activities. Birthday parties, weddings, Thanksgiving, Christmas. And by 'incessantly' I mean they videotaped them in their entirety, accumulating, I imagine, hour upon hour upon hour of "Happy birthday, to you" and everyone sharing what they're thankful for, and did you see that crazy sweater Aunt Jo made for little Timmy? Adorable.

In Borges's "Universal History of Infamy," there's a short fragment at the end recounting a fabled Empire that elevated cartography to its highest form and exactitude. The map of a province was the size of a city, while the map of the Empire was the size of an entire province. Unsatisfied, they eventually crafted a map "that was of the same Scale as the Empire, and that coincided with it point for point." Later generations, however, judged such maps "cumbersome" and neglected both the study of cartography, abandoning these perfect maps altogether "to the Rigors of Sun and Rain." Today, "In the western Deserts, tattered Fragments of the Maps are still to be found, Sheltering an occasional Beast or Beggar."

Thinking about it, at what time would you take out a videotape of an entire birthday party and rewatch it? Or Thanksgiving? The Empire's map seems crude child's play next to such a library. And what kind of interest could there be in two hours of something you routinely reenacted? It's like all you've done is over-produced a prop for a made for television movie about a family that loses a member at a tragic age or is affected badly by a divorce due to emotional carelessness. Now, there's mom, make-up smeared, drunkenly watching a flickering screen as poor taken-from-us-too-soon Timmy, still in that adorable little sweater, gives Aunt Jo a kiss.

Worse yet, what if videotaping every moment of your life somehow created a completely alternative life, one that existed entirely in magnetic patterns on ribbons of polyethylene terephthalate? And rather than being a static recording, it communed with its subjects, reshaping the recorded visual images to the contours of our subsequent interior lives? There's mom, her mascara streaked, over-filled goblet of chardonnay in hand, cowering in darkness as the screen confirms that, yes, Dan, her ex-husband, was a jerk all those years, even back then when Timmy (God rest his soul) was only ten and Dan left the birthday party early just to play golf with his buddies. A child's tenth birthday comes only once, memories last a lifetime, a father should be there for his children. How could she not have seen it? What a jerk Dan is. What a fool she was. *Sips wine*

Of course, Dan didn't golf, not then, not ever. But now, having finally watched that tape, she arrives at McDonald's for the weekly pick-up of Timmy (he lives in this version and is twelve) and she notices that Dan is wearing golf clothes and seems eager to leave. Probably just can't wait to get back to that golf course and all those jerk friends of his.

The pernicious effect of the tape has expanded, extending its visual image past the interior to the field of her entire life and to everyone who inhabits that field. Did Dan have these jerk friends? No. But he does now, just like he has that terrible girlfriend, the stupid car, the [insert thing that confirms and extends her bad opinion of Dan, of herself, etc.].

Nostalgia. From Greek "nostos," a return to one's home, and "algia," pain. These videotapes, these new, morphing maps of the past that shape the present, lend a veracity to nostalgia's true origins unlike our current sense of the word since entirely verifiable ("It's right there on the tape; why didn't I notice it then?"). But they are entirely false and therefore consonant with our current notions of nostalgia, especially any nostalgia attached to a craze. A craze invariably proceeds by disabling memory, if not simply misremembering, then unremembering. There is a subtle drama in merely forgetting that leaves a sense of loss, say, the pathos of an aging mother not recognizing her daughter. Unremembering replaces it with a seamless if harsh traverse. The sterility of a senile woman meeting a younger one; the older one never had children, and the other was abandoned as an infant. Gone is the implication that this senile woman abandoned her child at birth, that this younger woman was drawn by the gravity of fate to meet her unrecognized mother. Unremembering permits no irony, dramatic or otherwise.

The possibility of this videotaped world distortion, this unseen magic that a library of video tapes could impose on the world, suggests something about the things we would save from a burning house. More acutely, it changes the thoughts we have about what we might save from a burning house. The house has not burned down, so we project ourselves into one of several futures. One is hurried, chaotic. An alarm rings its jarring buzz. We awaken in the dark to the smell of smoke and scurry, then stagger, for an exit, thinking only then to grab that photograph from the nightstand.

Another is cooler, emotionally misty, an imaginary place beyond disaster. We contemplate the things we treasure there, back in the now from which we launched ourselves. How grand I will feel if I save things when my house burns down. I will sit on a swinging chair in my new home, filled with the satisfaction that I chose to save this thing from that other, burning-down house.

We could make this routine, an exercise in planning. Here is the list of things I would save from my burning house. I will place those things here, in this chute. At the first sign of fire, they will be ejected to a place of safety. For the remainder of my existence, they will stay there, in the chute, unless of course my house burns down. It never burns down. I die and am cremated, but those things remain in their chute.

Yet another is aleatory, a game of chance. I will save this thing from my burning house (that old pair of glasses or that clock, the one with the cat's eyes going back and forth as the tail swishes) and this or that is the reason for saying "I will save this thing from my burning house." My house burns down. There is regret. How could I not have saved that small gold locket with the photograph inside, a small face of someone I loved cut into the same heart shape as the locket itself? But am I merely thinking about that future or am I in it? Or am I thinking about waking up to the sound of the smoke alarm?

There are more. As I think of what I will save from my burning house, I am now regarding all things as things I must think about saving from my burning house. That is a new, unending test for each thing and a noble labor for me. Hercules had his stables. I have everything I could possibly save from my burning house and a new, unremitting judgment imposed on the material world. But, unlike the damning thumb of Caesar, its imperial distance owing nothing to anyone, not even the booing or cheering crowd, everything is damned to the flames unless I act, even if that act is just the salvation of the thought "I would save you from my burning house." I, too, am plagued. Once a light cloak, the material world has become an iron cage, or perhaps more accurately the cloak of Nessus, a deceitful comfort now a poisonous membrane.

Perhaps worse, what if I refuse to consider what to save from my burning house and then, since I'm lazy or at least lack mental inertia, the call to do so weakens, wanes, and then fades completely. I become not detached so much as disinterested in "things." This shirt, those books, that stuffed animal, all things transmuted under the weight of their sameness. Perhaps the shirt has little teddy bears printed all over it. The book is "The Teddy Bears' Picnic." The teddy bear is wearing a shirt and reading a little book. It's not a weight after all, this material world, but an amusingly bland lightness. Things begin to float. I begin to float. The fire spreads through the super-heated air, arcs of searing flame consuming everything. The world fades to ash.

Mother's Home by the Sea

Felix Isar stared at the letter he was holding. He didn't remember his mother, not really. She had died almost twenty-five years ago, when he was six months old. He remembered her the way you remember someone telling you a story. He knew the photographs of her, the bookcases filled with her scholarly papers, the jewelry box with the strange ring he planned to use for his engagement to Sophie.

The letter was a surprise.

"I didn't know either," his father said. "But here we are. You own a house, I guess."

"I've never even heard of New Weymouth," Felix said.

"It's in Massachusetts," his father said. "On the coast. About seven hours up I-95. She told me she grew up there, that her parents were dead."

"But why did she have a house there?"

"I don't know. Honestly, I had no idea. She was from Massachusetts; her parents were dead. That's all she said about it. She didn't like to talk about the past. Maybe it's a family home. The letter says something about you turning twenty-five."

In 2019, Felix Isar graduated from the New York Institute of Technology with a degree in architecture and urban design. Now, he had a job with the City of Baltimore renovating affordable housing down in Fells Point. He was an affable young man, slight of build with an easy laugh and an unpretentious manner. He was a talented architect, dedicated to his work and helpful without the artistic vanity that haunted his profession or the cutthroat indifference of property developers. He was a natural fit in the world of non-profits and government agencies.

More than talent, Felix had a child-like curiosity, which made everything new and interesting. He was constantly experimenting with food, listening to music, and reading all kinds of books. He had taught himself to draw and paint with watercolors. He visited graveyards and art museums and traveled to cities to explore their public transit. He was the sort of person who would read about converting a Nintendo Gameboy into a chip-tune synthesizer, and then actually do it. And, with the summer drawing to a close, the prospect of exploring this strange inheritance and New Weymouth was an easy excuse to get out of the swelter of Baltimore for a few weeks.

Felix left on Thursday, hoping to avoid any of the weekend traffic to Cape Cod. As he approached New Weymouth, he left the interstate, driving along the winding coast road past a series of coves and daunting cliffs. Run-down seaside cottage rentals dotted the hills, and there were several congested collections of buildings along the way, small grocery stores and glum looking restaurants with large signs advertising lobster. About ten miles from town, the terrain flattened and the road passed through salt marshes, a sea of grass waving over brackish water. Just when he started to feel lost, the road turned left, a thin line of asphalt between the marshes and the ocean's shimmering glass.

The low, worn profile of New Weymouth sprawled in front of him. The outskirts were mostly dilapidated houses on treeless streets with abandoned telephone poles and the occasional car parked with a tire or two over the curb. He saw a few children playing a nameless game, but they scurried off as he drove by. In one house, he could swear someone pulled the blinds down at his approach. There was a once fine old house surrounded by an iron spiked fence, but the broken shutters and overgrown lawn betrayed its ruin. Gradually, signs of dim life appeared, and the town proper coalesced. There was another lobster restaurant, a particularly large and respectable looking one with a big sign that read "The Reel Delite." It featured a fiberglass mermaid on the roof, her well-rouged cheeks cracked and peeling. It had a parking lot dedicated to tourist buses, and an old pier jutting into the water, bleached from age and reeking of creosote. A hulking old hotel perched along the waterfront on the other side, its elegant facade sagging in spots and defaced by a modern sign with flickering lights that read "Motor Lodge."

The lawyer's office was in a strip mall just outside the town center, next door to a beauty salon and a tattoo parlor. The lawyer was a corpulent man of uncertain age with thick glasses and a wide belt that he constantly tugged on while standing to keep his pants up.

"Don Miller," he said, extending a pudgy hand garnished with a pinky ring. "Let's get you sorted out."

The office was a single room, with a chrome-legged desk, two chairs with faded upholstery, and a single framed diploma on the wall.

"Just sign here, here, and here," he said, arranging documents on the desk. "I'll get the keys. Insurance runs for another month. And this is Mrs. Latham's phone number."

"Mrs. Latham?" Felix said looking up from the papers.

"Your tenant," the lawyer said. "There's no lease, just month to month. Shouldn't be a problem. Always pays her rent, but if you want her out, that's fine, too. She's been living there since who knows when, but there's plenty of other places. Retired schoolteacher. A good tenant. Knew your mother."

"What is the rent?"

"Well," the lawyer said, "it's $300. That's low. Very low, especially if you think about what the whole house could go for. She was living there when I got the file, and I thought it would be a mistake to change anything. You know, for insurance and such. Hard to insure an empty house."

"I never knew about this," Felix said, gesturing at the documents. "My father didn't know either. How long did my mother own this house?"

"I don't know much about that," Miller said. "This file came with the practice. Here, let me show you." He turned to the solitary filing cabinet and rummaged for a moment. "It's a family home, though," he said over his shoulder. "Your grandparents lived there."

He plopped a disordered file on the desk.

"That's the whole thing," he said. "You can have it, if you want. Not much in there. I don't need it anymore."

Felix scooped up the brown folder. A photograph slipped out. It was a single figure at a distance, slightly out of focus, a young woman standing in front of a white building. Something dangled down at the top of the frame. It was the tail of the mermaid at The Reel Delite. He studied it carefully before slipping it back in.

The house sat on top of a solitary hill at the edge of the town center, looking south towards the water. It was surrounded by large trees that hid its Queen Anne niceties: the square tower with overhanging eaves, the patchwork of wood and brick, and the broad porch with an imposing pediment and columns. It was almost fair to call it a mansion, except there was restraint in its flourishes, and also an eyesore fire escape that climbed its right side to a gabled window on the third floor. Mrs. Latham's window, he presumed.

Miller had said that Mrs. Latham only rented the top floor, which included a small attic. The house had not been divided into apartments, and the only concession to its rental status was the fire escape and a small kitchen in her rooms. While she did not use the remainder of the house, her cats roamed freely.

Felix debated whether he should knock on the big double front doors or simply enter, but before he could decide he heard someone coming down the stairs. The knob turned slowly, and the door swung open.

"Good afternoon," a slight woman of uncertain age said, a large black cat lying serenely in her arms. "You must be Felix."

"Yes," Felix said. "Hello. Mrs. Latham, I presume. I'm Felix Isar."

"Come in, come in," she said stepping back and nodding her head in the direction of the large front parlor. "You must be tired from your drive."

They stepped into the parlor. It was filled with large, over-stuffed furniture. Indistinct paintings covered the walls, dark with lacquer and age. Most were seascapes, with the largest depicting a clipper ship heavy with sail. Over an impressive fireplace hung a faded mirror with a heavy gilt frame, and beneath it a white marble clock ticked on the mantel next to a statuette of Venus doting over a cherub. Federal style pewter candlesticks with long beeswax candles stood guard on either side. The floor was almost entirely covered with an enormous Savonnerie rug patterned with pears and pheasants that, while clearly showing signs of age, remained vibrantly colorful. The entire effect of the setting felt antique and disused, but clean and well-maintained.

Felix stopped to look around, but Mrs. Latham continued out of the room through a swinging door. The cat jumped from her arms and ran away. "I'll get some tea," she said on the way out.

They sat together on the sofa and drank tea from red teacups laced with gold in a Chinese design. Felix sipped politely. The saucer tinkled like glass when he put down his cup.

"Mrs. Latham," Felix began, "I'm not exactly sure—"

"Kimberly, please," Mrs. Latham said.

"Kimberly," Felix said. "I didn't even know I owned this house until a few days ago, and, well, I'm not sure what I'm going to do with it."

"That's all right," Mrs. Latham said. "I know, what you're thinking. It was an unusual arrangement, my staying here. Don't give it another thought. I can move easily enough."

"No, that's not it," Felix said. "Honestly. I have no idea whether I'm going to keep it, sell it, or what. For now, of course you can stay. I'm trying to find out how my mother fits into all this."

"She was a lovely girl," Mrs. Latham said.

"You knew my mother?"

"Of course, sweetheart," Mrs. Latham said, putting a hand over his. "That's why I'm here. Didn't Mr. Miller explain anything?"

"The Lawyer? No. No, I just signed some things, got the keys. He did mention you were renting. That's about it."

"Well, to be fair, he didn't know your mother. He bought old Matthew Johnson's practice. Matthew passed away last month. Miller isn't from here. He's from Worcester, I think. Not much of a lawyer, I'm afraid, but there's not much call for them here."

"Please, tell me about her," Felix said.

"She was my student," she said, "and a very good one. Probably my best. The only one who ever became a professor, as far as I know."

"And the house?"

"This was your grandparents' house," she said. "And your great grandparents' house. I'm not sure before that. It's at least one hundred years old, probably older. It should be on the historical register, but New Weymouth is one of those places people would like to forget about. Yours is one of the oldest families. Well, the oldest that still has living members."

"Wait," Felix said, fumbling in the file for the photograph. "Do you recognize her."

"Of course," Mrs. Lambeth said, holding it at arm's length. "That's your mother. She waited tables there in the summer."

"Waited tables?"

"Yes, at The Reel Delite," she said. "Your grandparents owned it. See, there's the tail of the mermaid. Despite the name, it was a fine restaurant back then. They had their own boat. Gary Boudreaux used to fish for them. The fresh catch was always the best in town."

"What happened to them?" Felix said. "My grandparents."

"You really don't know anything, poor child," she said.

"No, I don't," he said. "My mother told my father that her parents were dead. He knows about New Weymouth, well, at least that my mother was from here, but that's it. He never visited."

"Well, if you go down there, to The Reel Delite," she said, "you'll see a lot of history on the walls. There're all kinds of photographs still up. Your grandparents posing with famous guests, that kind of thing. It's all a bit kitschy now, with the tourists, but back then it was a nice place, and they gave it a personal touch. Folks came from Boston and Providence. Stayed in the Monmouth Arms, that big hotel on the water next door. The hotel never bothered with a bar or restaurant. The guests just went to The Reel Delite. Suited everyone. There was a little garden between them where they would string lights and throw dances all summer. It was wonderful there, by the seashore on a summer night, listening to music and the sounds of the sea all mixed together."

Mrs. Lambeth got a soft, faraway look in her eyes for a moment.

"Your grandparents," she said, coming back. "They were lost at sea, I'm sorry to say."

"A storm?"

"No, it was quite a mystery," she said. "Gary came in to take the boat out, very early in the morning, you know, and it was gone. Coast Guard found it off Naushon Island that same day, no one on board. Rogue wave or something criminal, perhaps. Broke your mother's heart. She left a month later and, well, the rest is history. But she kept this place for you. She wanted you to have a choice in the matter."

"So, you've been living here for over twenty years?"

"Twenty-five," Mrs. Latham said, "but they tell us the universe is roughly thirteen billion years old. My time here is the smallest grain of sand on the largest beach."

Felix took the front room on the second floor, with windows on two sides. He could see down the hill to the waterfront in the old part of town, where white-sided derelict warehouses stood with lobster pots lined the docks stacked in neat squares ready to be loaded. The room had wainscoting topped by a chair rail and the rest of the walls were papered with a nautical pattern of mermaids floating in delicate seaweed. He threw his suitcase on the bed and decided to completely unpack. Then he explored the house.

The rest of the second floor consisted of two bedrooms, a small den or sewing room, a walk-in closet with intricate shelving for linens and tablecloths, and an enormous bathroom. The bathtub was made of brass, with eagle claw feet, a teak handrail, and a decorative pendant with a circular handle. On the first floor, other than the front room, the kitchen had a butler's pantry and two boxy sinks with zinc lining. There was a library filled with floor to ceiling books shelves and a sliding ladder. Adjacent was a study with heavy drapes that billowed around the windows, and a broad, round table in the middle with a hanging overhead light under an elaborate shade. Six leather armchairs surrounded it.

The basement was walled with smooth stones, wide and empty, matching the footprint of the house, except at the back where it seemed to jut out at least ten feet into an unlighted rectangle where the walls were rough and chiseled. Grabbing a flashlight, Felix looked in and noticed a large, green metal plate on the floor with a handle pull on one end. He'd have to ask Mr. Lambert—Kimberly, he corrected himself—about it.

Kimberly made dinner, fish chowder, which was surprisingly good. "The secret is the salt pork," she said, smiling at Felix's appetite. "Bacon won't do. Also, chives, which grow quite well in the garden."

"That bathtub is something," Felix said. "It's as big as a hot tub."

"Devil to keep clean," Kimberly said. "I polish it on rainy days. Something to do."

After dinner, Felix walked around the neighborhood. The house sat alone on its verdant hill, but a few blocks away the town was mostly run-down four-story buildings, empty store fronts, and an old movie theater, the trim lights on its triangular marquee flashing dimly. In a small square, an old church with dark windows sulked, its red door's paint peeling. There was a separate entrance to a half-sunk basement with what looked like a small Masonic emblem on the door. The windows peaking up from brick wells glowed a dull blue.

Felix saw a few small storefront bars that looked a little rough around the edges, but he finally found a large restaurant set on its own lot, The Reef Steakhouse, and he could see a long well-stocked bar and good lighting. It seemed like a safe bet. He took a stool at the end and the bartender, a short man with an oddly narrow head and small nose, shuffled over and nodded wordlessly.

"I'll have a beer, please," Felix said. "Something local if you've got it."

"Seafoam," the bartender said, his eyes bulging for emphasis. "It's an IPA. People say they like it."

"Sounds great."

The beer was actually good, and the strangely saline aftertaste added something to it.

"You from around here?" the bartender asked, quietly polishing a glass. "You look a bit like you're from around here."

"Me?" Felix said. "No, no. I'm from Baltimore. My mother grew up here. Maybe you knew her. Beverly Marsh."

"A lot of Marsh folk around here," the bartender said, nodding his head slowly. "I got a cousin named Marsh. Never heard of Beverly Marsh, but I'm a young one, only thirty."

The bartender's eyes bulged again as he spoke, and Felix thought the man looked almost fifty years old.

"You got the look," the bartender said. "She gave you just enough, I suppose."

It was a bright morning, cool and breezy, and Felix went down to the waterfront right after breakfast. The lobster pots from the night before were gone, and there was only one fishing boat left in the harbor, an old Cape Dory bobbing lazily with the engine idling. A fisherman walking along the quay in oilskins holding a bucket in each hand passed by, nodded and winked at Felix, and hopped on board, whistling a nameless tune.

"You thinking about fishing?" he yelled to Felix, his voice oddly musical.

"No, just out for a walk," Felix said.

"I can take you out," the fisherman said. "Nothing like a day on the water. Always use the company."

"Thank you," Felix said, "but I'm not much of a fisherman."

The man eyed Felix carefully as he emptied the buckets into the bait well.

"For all that, you look like one," the man said, and winked as he began to whistle again.

At 10:00, Felix drove to The Reel Delite. The parking lot was empty, but the door was unlocked and he went in. The lights were off, and the dining room loomed in still darkness, dozens of tables already set with glinting tableware and water glasses. Something banged out of sight, and a sturdy young woman in a server's uniform wearing white shoes burst through the kitchen's double doors.

"Oh, hello," she said cheerfully. "A bit early for lunch, I'm afraid. I can get you coffee, though."

"I'm Beverly Marsh's son," Felix said, awkwardly. "Her parents used to own this place."

"Beverly Marsh," the woman said. "I knew her. When I was a wee one, of course. Sure, everyone knew them. I think we're related. Do you know Alanis Allen? She's my cousin. She married a Marsh. Ezekiel or Ezra. Something biblical. Poor girl. He drowned last year. Fishing is a tough life."

"No, I don't know anyone," Felix stumbled. "I mean, I don't know my mother's family. She died when I was baby."

"Sorry to hear that," the woman said. "How can I help you?"

"Well, I inherited a house," Felix said, "and the woman living there—"

"Oh, Mrs. Latham," the woman said. "That makes sense. Taught high school English. That's quite a house."

"How did you know?" Felix said, laughing.

"This is a small town," she said. "Not many houses here to inherit, not many worth anything, anyway. That's the old Marsh house, one of the oldest that we got, near Fletcher Square and the old church. That house has a lot of history."

"Yes, it does," Felix said. "That's why I'm here. Mrs. Latham said there are photos of my mother and grandparents here."

"Lots of them," the woman said, nodding to the far wall. "They're everywhere. You want to take a look? Wait, I'll get the lights." She swerved past Felix and ducked behind the bar. The lights went on.

"You take a look around," she said. "No rush. You need anything, just give a shout. My name is Allie." And she padded off, back into the kitchen.

The photographs were mostly 8 x 10, tanned smiling tourists in casual handshakes at tables, group shots under the leering mermaid, sunsets on the dock. Two people appeared in most of them, an older couple with good-natured smiles, and he assumed they were his grandparents. His grandfather always leaned over in a practiced way, turning to the camera, while his grandmother stood to the side, both with comfortably smiling faces. There were a few real celebrities, movie stars from the 1960s and 70s, and even one with Joe Namath. Most were anonymous tourists, but well-dressed and polished. It gave Felix a strange nostalgia for something he'd never known, but there wasn't much real history of the place. The photographs needed someone who was there, narrating the scene.

"You want to see the old ones?" Allie shouted from the bar. "I can open up the banquet room for you." Before Felix could respond, she was rushing through the tables towards the back of the restaurant. He followed. "There's some really old stuff back here, from the olden timey days."

She unlocked a set of double doors and held it open for Felix. The room was almost as big as the main one, but the tables and chairs were stored to one side. The entire back wall was windows with a view of the short pier and the harbor beyond. Allie pointed to a glass case to the right.

"These things," she said as they walked, "come from the old town, when the gold refinery was still running. It was a wild place back then. Lots of money changing hands. They say fish would swim right up into the harbor."

The photos showed somber faced man in stiff suits posed in groups. Some wore sashes with the Masonic symbol on them.

"What's that mean?" Felix said. "Were they Masons?"

"Some kind of local fraternity," Allie said. "They still have it, but I don't know anyone who is actually in it. It's not Masons or Elks or whatever. Something else, to do with the fishermen, I think. See, look there."

Felix leaned closer. The symbol did look roughly like the Masonic square and compass, but only in outline. It had some strange design inside it, perhaps a fish or a man.

"Here's another one," Allie said.

This photo was of a man sitting in an ornate chair, with two others behind. They all had the sash on, and the seated man was wearing something like an outlandishly ornate crown or diadem. The band around his forehead was a complicated geometric design, but over his head it rose into fingers or spines, decorated with barely discernible figures. The entire effect was unsettling enough, but worse yet were the men's faces. The eyes bulged, even more than the bartender's last night, and their faces seemed inhumanly thin.

"It's funny how people look so different in old photos sometimes," Allie said.

"It sure is," Felix said. "It's like the world was black and white back then."

As they walked back to the front, Felix remembered the photo of his mother.

"Do you recognize her?" he asked.

"I think so," Allie said. "I think that's her. You could take a look at the high school yearbooks if you'd like. They've got all of them at the town library. Mr. Allen, the librarian, knows local history, too. How long are you staying?"

"I haven't decided what to do with the house," Felix said. "At least a week."

"Well, if you're looking for something to do, we have a sunset booze cruise every Saturday during the summer. Leaves right from the pier. Six o'clock. Bring Mrs. Latham along, lots of folks be glad to see her."

The library was a historic Carnegie library, well made of stone and brick with an arched entryway and green slate roof. Inside, a dignified looking man in a tan sweater vest and white shirt stood behind a desk. He was taking books from one stack, opening them, stamping the inside cover, and placing them on another stack. He looked up over reading glasses as Felix approached.

"May I help you?" he said, in soft voice.

"My name is Felix," Felix said. "I'm visiting New Weymouth for the first time. My mother was Beverly Marsh."

"A Marsh?" the man said. "Practically royalty."

"Hardly," Felix said. "I never knew her or any of my family here, but I would have known about royal blood. I was told you have the high school yearbooks."

"The Marsh family is as old as the town," the man said. "Back to 1810. Back in the Innsmouth days."

"Innsmouth?"

"New Weymouth's original name," the man said. "Prosperous fishing town, gold refinery. It was never much to look at, but it had some finer points aside from commerce. The Marsh house, of course, that's a fine house. And the church on Fletcher Square, while modest, is historically significant. The old wharf is run down now, but in its heyday it was a hub for commerce. Innsmouth ships sailed all over the world, as far as the Pacific and Asia."

"Really?" Felix said.

"Excuse me," the man said, extending a hand. "Herbert Allen. Call me Herb. My family has been here a long time, too, but not nearly in such a distinguished way. Mrs. Latham still living in the Marsh House?"

"Yes, she is," Felix said. "I inherited it, and I'm not sure what I'm going to do with it. Do you mind me asking about this?"

"Mind? To the contrary. I love to talk about New Weymouth. There's more to it than meets the eye. Much more."

"At The Reel Delite," Felix said, "there are photos, in the back. Old ones with Masons or something. I saw their lodge in the basement of the church, I think."

"The Esoteric Order of Dagon," Herb said. "That's from Innsmouth. All the men who worked for your family since the time of Obed Marsh belonged. Nowadays it has only a handful of members, mostly a social club."

"Obed Marsh," Felix said. "How far back does he go?"

"Well, your grandfather, I assume, was Randall Marsh. He was the son of Barnabas Marsh, whose father was Onesiphorus. Obed Marsh was his father. Obed was a trader, built the town."

"So that would be my great-great-great-grandfather."

"Yes," Mr. Allen said. "The maternal side of your family is less clear, not that it matters much anymore. The Marsh women were quite private. Something to do with society, I suppose. Kept to themselves.

"As for history, Obed brought the gold refinery to Innsmouth back in the 1820s. Traded extensively in the South Pacific. There was some trouble with neighboring towns in the 1840s, and he was jailed briefly. I think it had to do with commercial rivalries. He died 1878. Onesiphorus took over until his death in 1910. Barnabas was unfortunately killed in 1927."

"Killed?" Felix said. "As in 'murdered?'"

"No, it was during the prohibition raids," Herb said. "FBI came in and there was a gun battle at the warehouses. Not uncommon, bootlegging and that kind of thing. Ships came down from Canada, unloaded at night. By that time, prohibition was already strongly opposed by much of the public, so the raid on Innsmouth was an effort by the government to shore things up. But it went badly, and many people were killed. The feds even blew up the old reef. Claimed it had a secret cache in the caves, but I don't think that was true. It was a show of force."

"So, they just changed the name?"

"Yes, it's what passed for a cover-up. There was a mass migration after the raid, with only a few old timers remaining behind. The government changed the name, thought perhaps people would forget the history, too. History lives on, though. You're living proof, a descendant of Obed Marsh, in the flesh. It's quite wonderful, I think. If you'd like, I have written a short book on the town's history. Let me get you a copy."

Herb returned from his office with a small book open to the flyleaf.

"Here," he said, picking up a pen. "Your own copy of 'Local Color: New Weymouth and Old Innsmouth.' 'To Felix, descendant of Obed Marsh, warmly, Herb Allen'. Keep it. Lord knows, you might actually read it."

"The woman at The Reel Delite mentioned the high school yearbooks," Felix said, leafing through the book.

"Oh, you'd like to see your mother," Herb said. "Of course. Over here. Now, do you know what year she graduated?"

"She was born in 1965."

"Let's try 1983, then."

Herb pulled the book down, flipped through, and held it open for Felix.

"Each senior was given a full page," Herb said. "It's a small town, so plenty of room."

The photograph was a posed studio shot, his mother sitting on a stool wearing a skirt and sweater, hair pulled back in a ponytail. Her hands covered one knee, and she tilted her head, smiling. She looked young, but somehow older than eighteen. The opposite entry, a slender faced boy with drooping eyes named Linnet Marsh, had a similar photo, and the usual notes next to his name. "Thanks to all my friends. Track and Marching Band forever." His mother's notes consisted of a poem that took up three quarters of the page. It was "The World Below the Brine," by Walt Whitman:

The World Below the Brine

Forests at the bottom of the sea, the branches and leaves,

Sea-lettuce, vast lichens, strange flowers and seeds, the thick tangle, openings, and pink turf,

Different colors, pale gray and green, purple, white, and gold, the play of light through the water,

Dumb swimmers there among the rocks, coral, gluten, grass, rushes, and the aliment of the swimmers,

Sluggish existences grazing there suspended, or slowly crawling close to the bottom,

The sperm-whale at the surface blowing air and spray, or disporting with his flukes,

The leaden-eyed shark, the walrus, the turtle, the hairy sea-leopard, and the sting-ray,

Passions there, wars, pursuits, tribes, sight in those ocean-depths, breathing that thick-breathing air, as so many do,

The change thence to the sight here, and to the subtle air
breathed by beings like us who walk this sphere,

The change onward from ours to that of beings who walk
other spheres.

"She became a professor of English, correct?" Herb said. "Well, you
can see she had the inclination. Most people don't leave this place, and
no one becomes a professor. Except your mother."

Felix fell asleep with Allen's book tented on his chest. He dreamed
of the green metal plate in the basement, its rusted edges and flaking
galvanic corrosion. Pulling at the handle, it swung open and clanged to
the floor. Below, spiral stairs descended, carved into the rock. Far down
dim light flickered as he spun into the earth, deeper and deeper. Then
he was in a wide space, an enormous, unsounded distance on all sides,
and water, cool, still, and black. Something moving, coming towards
him, shapeless and soundless, rearing above the surface, a pulsing bulk
with floating eyes, blinking, staring eyes shifting in the dark. Beyond, a
sinister chorus hovered in the blackness.

He startled awake, the book falling to the floor. Checking the
clock, it was 3:13 AM. He lay fitfully dozing for hours until the hazy
dawn awakened him.

"It's remarkable," Mrs. Latham said after Felix told her about the
visit to The Reel Delite and the library. "Your mother told none of this
to your father."

"Nope," Felix said. "I was going to call him, but I don't want him to
think I'm angry or upset. I'm just mystified. By the way, do you know
what's under that green trapdoor in the basement?"

"Trapdoor?" she said. "I'm not sure what you mean."

"There's a green trapdoor on the far side of the basement, in the
floor. A service hatch or something."

"I couldn't say," Mrs. Latham said. "You should be careful, though.
Lord knows, this is an old house. At some point they even had asbestos

down there. You know, those little tiles? Cost a fortune to remove them."

"It's a strange feeling," Felix said. "Grandparents I never knew. A family that built a town. Bootleggers. An ancestor who sailed around the world."

"Don't forget the mothers," Mrs. Latham said. "The women of the town don't show up much in the history books, but they had secret lives. They kept this place civilized as best they could."

"Of course," Felix said. "There's so much I don't know. I want to figure it out, figure *this* out." He gestured at the house around them. "Have you ever heard of The Esoteric Order of Dagon?"

"Those old farts?" she said. "Of course. They sit around drinking and playing cards."

"And you must know about Innsmouth," Felix said.

"I do," she said, "the old name for New Weymouth. The town almost died out after the government raid. Well, that's what my mother said. But enough people stayed, figured the world would forget the old ways of Innsmouth. That's when tourism picked up. Innsmouth was a booming place, but it was no place for outsiders. Your grandparents knew that. They kept things alive here, in New Weymouth, when it seemed like no one would give the town a second chance. It's still not much of a town, but it has some charm if you know where to look."

"Allie invited me to the booze cruise tonight," Felix said. "Well, 'invited' is a bit strong. She mentioned it to me and said that you should come along."

"Oh, I don't know," Mrs. Latham said. "Is it still pirate themed?"

"No, it's just a sunset cruise," Felix said, taking out his phone. "Here, let's see if it's online. There, The Reel Delite Sunset Cruise. That looks like a nice boat."

Felix held out his phone. There was a picture of a stout nosed boat with square windows on the enclosed first deck and an open deck above it with a blue awning.

"That's the old ferry to Naushon Island," she said. "It's not a nice boat. But it's seaworthy. Used to run that line in all weather."

"I think it looks nice and I think we should go."

"I'll think about," Mrs. Latham said. "We'll have dinner early. I'll give Allie a ring later."

Felix decided to explore New Weymouth more thoroughly, heading away from the faded blocks around Fletcher square, down Federal Street, south towards the river. An old footbridge with questionable wooden planks crossed a gorge with a waterfall. Children were swimming in the roiling pools below, easily slipping in and out, dashing over boulders and diving under fallen logs. There were no adults around, and Felix wondered at the casual way anyone would let children so young play in obvious danger. On the other side, the road turned, and he came upon an abandoned industrial site, comprised mostly of a hulking brick building with an enormous chimney. Again, children scampered through the detritus, playing, carefree and unsupervised.

The town petered out here, so he turned back and followed a path along the river, through the overgrown backyards of houses similar to those he'd seen on his drive in. Once fine houses were decayed, some tilting threateningly on their foundations or dangling a shutter here and there. All the houses had drapes or blinds closed, and when he came to a derelict church with a blasted steeple, he could have sworn someone was looking out at him from the side window. Depressed by this part of town, he turned back, crossed the bridge, and took Federal Street until it crossed Fish Street, which ran down to the waterfront.

The ancient wharves here were empty, except near the marine mechanics, where an enormous lift was hauling a fishing boat up out of the water. The men were almost all shorter than normal, with the bartender's thin head and staring expression, but friendly. They nodded and went about their business in the stalwart way of New Englanders, joking with each other. Many were wearing heavy shirts and watch caps, despite the heat, and a fire crackled in an unattended oil barrel. Felix turned to walk out past the warehouses.

"Mind yourself, sir," a man yelled without menace, his voice oddly thick. "There's forklifts getting ready for the fleet. You'll not want to be out there then. Get knocked right over. You want to look around, you should step out there on the old pier. You'll get a good view of the harbor. No one will mind if you do." He gestured towards a single pier that ran out in front of the repair shop.

Standing at the end of it, Felix could see the entire harbor: The Reel Delite, the hotel, and the marina one way, and the commercial wharves and warehouses the other, all the way down to the tidy tourist shops in the town center near the breakwater. Boats were passing the harbor mouth in a line at the seaward end of the harbor.

"That's where the reef was," said the man, coming up behind Felix. "That red buoy, with the number 5 on it. Still a shallow spot on a low tide. Always got to look out for that."

"I heard about it," Felix said, "from Mr. Allen. The librarian. Something about bootleggers and prohibition."

"Ain't no bootleggers," the man said. "They just wanted people out of Innsmouth. I guess they figured it would ruin the fishing."

"You know about Innsmouth?"

"Everybody knows about Innsmouth," the man said. "Everybody that lives here, anyway. They just don't want to talk about it."

"If it wasn't bootlegging," Felix said, "what was it? Smuggling?"

"You could call it smuggling," the man said. "More like trading, if you know what I mean."

Felix shook his head and shrugged.

"Exchange," the man said. "Gold and such. You wouldn't believe what Yankee traders got up to. They say the reef came up twenty feet above water at a low tide." He winked and nodded. "You take care," he added, and waddled away.

When Felix returned to the house, Mrs. Latham was in the kitchen, emptying the cabinets on to a worn wooden table. Pots and pans were stacked at one end, and dry goods filled several cardboard boxes. A bamboo spice rack lay flat, its small shelves jammed with unlabeled jars half full of faded contents. She turned in surprise.

"Oh, my," she said. "I thought you wouldn't be back until supper."

"We have the sunset cruise," Felix said. "Remember?"

"Yes, yes," she said, snatching up a broom and sweeping distractedly. "I talked to Allie. I haven't forgotten, just wanted to get things tidy before we went."

"Let me get that," Felix said, taking the broom from her. "You really shouldn't bother with this. I'll get someone in to clean things up."

"I just wanted to get things tidy," she said again, "before we go. Just something to keep busy."

Felix watched her flit around the room, surprised at her agility. She pulled a chair over to the counter and started to climb up.

"Please," he said. "Let me get that."

But she stepped up quickly, grabbing a large, enameled casserole from the top shelf.

"No worries," she said, stepping down and putting the pot on the table. "You might have a yard sale. It would be a nice way to meet folks in the neighborhood. They're not many, but enough, and everyone likes a yard sale."

"Mrs. Latham," Felix said. "Kimberly. You don't have to move out. Even if I kept the place and moved in, I wouldn't ask you to move out. The more I learn about this town and this house, the less I want to even think about selling it. There's so much history here, and my mother's family—my family is a big part of that."

Mrs. Latham stopped and watched Felix's face, a still expression passing over her features, as if listening to distant music or the low horn of a ship borne over the fog.

"Yes," she said, dreamily, her voice soft, "so much history."

She placed her hands in the pockets of her apron, thought better of it and untied the apron, turning to hang it on the back of a chair.

"You think you might stay?" she said, the slightest glimmer of hope far beneath the surface.

"Well," Felix said, "no, not as things are. I've only just seen the place. I don't know anything about it, and I've got a lot of work to do back in Baltimore. But there's no rush, and I'm not going to pretend there is."

"No rush," she repeated with a half-dreaming voice. "No rush at all." She grabbed the apron off the chair and balled it up, dropping it in a box. "Come. Let's sit down for a moment."

She pushed through the swinging door into the living room and let the door close behind her absentmindedly. Confused, Felix followed. Mrs. Latham stood limply next to the love seat.

"We should talk," she said, and half-flopped into the cushions.

"Are you all right?" Felix said, sitting next to her. She shook her head, a forgetful look in her eyes.

"I'm fine," she said, something like regret in her voice. "I need to tell you the truth. Your mother was my sister. I'm your aunt. I know, I know, I look so much older. And I am older, older than your mother, but not as old as you think. It's how things are in our family. Some of us... some of us just look older. We seem to age, but we aren't. We aren't aging."

Felix sat next to her, a look of delicate confusion creeping into his face.

"Kimberly," he said, "are you unwell? Let me call a doctor. Can I get you a glass of water?"

"No, thank you," she said, relief passing over her. "No. Did you hear me? I am your aunt."

"I know," Felix said. "It's a surprise, but why not tell me before? I'm even more confused."

"You mean, why did I lie? Go on, that's the truth of it. I lied to you. I've been lying for years. And so did your mother. Your father doesn't know I exist. He doesn't know anything about New Weymouth, the Marsh family."

"But why? Why keep this all from me? From him?"

"She didn't want you tangled up in all this," she said. "Not as a child. But now..." She trailed off, hesitant. "Now, things are different. You're grown, and you look so much like your mother. So much."

"You kept the house," Felix said. "For me."

"Yes," she said. "When Beverly left, she never wanted to come back. I stayed. There wasn't enough New Weymouth in her to keep her here. Not enough of the old Innsmouth. I had a life here, married, teaching. I like it here. She didn't. But she's given you a gift she wasn't sure she had. She's given you what she didn't have. This." She looked around the room and gestured with an outstretched arm. "It's a miracle, but she brought forth the old Marsh line once again in you."

"I don't understand. Why not just tell me? Why the lie about being her teacher?"

"No, that part is true," she said. "I'm ten years older than Beverly. And this is a small town. There was only one English teacher at the high school. She was my best student, that's the truth. She was made to leave this place. I was made to stay."

"You really do seem unwell," he said. "We'll skip the cruise. I'll make supper."

Kimberly put a hand on his.

"No," she said. "And look, it's almost six. Time to go. But one thing. Just say it once. I should very much like to hear you say it. Just call me 'Aunt Kimberly.'"

"Aunt Kimberly," Felix said, and she smiled.

They sat quietly for a few minutes.

"That cruise will do me good," she said. "And you can have dinner after at The Reel Delite. I haven't been there in ages. I'm sure you'll love it."

The parking lot was only half full, and a dozen or so people milled around the dock next to the boat, which bobbed gently against the pilings. Allie saw Felix and waved.

"We made it," he called through the car window. "I've got Aunt Kimberly with me."

"Oh, I know," Allie said, trotting over and leaning on the door sill. "She called last night. Good evening, Mrs. Latham. Everything's ready. Gary's captain, says he knows the best place to go, out by Naushon. He'll get us there as close to sunset as he can."

As Felix and Kimberly got out of the car, the small group of passengers in the parking lot parted, waiting for them. Kimberly boarded first, and a short, stout man with the narrow head and small nose rushed to help her.

"There's no need for any of that," she said, as he helped her up the gangway. "Not yet. I can still walk well enough."

On board, there was a small buffet with Swedish meatballs, crackers and cheese, and an open bar. Kimberly sat on a bench facing aft, where the cabin was open, gazing over the low gunwale at the swirling eddies from the engine's idle. Felix sat next to her, a bit uncomfortable so close to the aft opening.

"You're okay sitting here, Aunt Kimberly?" he said.

"You see those chains?" Kimberly said pointing to the safety barrier across the stern. "It's fine. Sitting here, you can feel free, watching the wake turn the water white and blue. I'd always sit here, those days when we took a picnic out to Naushon."

They cast off and the boat headed slowly down the pier, into the harbor's main channel, then turned towards the harbor mouth. Allie brought them gin and tonics and a plate of the meatballs.

"Oh, you remembered," Kimberly said. "These things are my favorite. And watch that drink, Felix. That's the strongest gin and tonic anywhere."

As they passed the harbor mouth, the red buoy by the old reef, its rusted sides bobbing in their wake, gave a sonorous clang from a bell inside its hull.

"If you come out here at low tide, in a small boat, mind you," Kimberly said, "ride over that and take a look. The reef is still there. They tried to get it all, but it goes down deep. They didn't even touch the far wall, I'm told."

The sun was threatening to touch the horizon, and the captain opened the throttle, the bow tipping up and chopping through the small waves. The wake bloomed behind the boat now, churning up like clouds before a storm. The engine noise and wind made it hard to hear.

"And you take all the time in the world with that house," Kimberly said. "You have the choice. Remember, that's all Beverly wanted, for you to have the choice."

They sat in silence as the boat sped along. Fifteen minutes later, it slowed, and turned sideways, pointed back towards shore. To the west, the sun hovered over the horizon, the dark shadows of islands and reaches of land solid against the constant liquid urges of the sea. Felix stood, and looked south at Naushon Island, blank and faceless as the sunset streaked the high points in a red fire of orange. Around the boat, it seemed, fish began to jump, only a few at first, then more and more, all coming towards them from Naushon.

"What's all that?" he said. "Is that how they feed?"

"They're running," Kimberly said.

"From what?" Felix said.

The people on the top deck were filing down the stairs, silent and somber, a young girl of no more than fourteen at the front. She held a single candle. Kimberly turned her head to watch. Abruptly, the fish stopped jumping, but there was something larger in the water, dolphins or seals perhaps. Felix leaned over and could see their shapes darting under and around the boat.

"Felix," Kimberly called to him. "It's time."

The girl walked aft and stood by the bench next to Kimberly, as the rest of the passengers formed a circle around the edges. She extended a hand to Kimberly, who stood and stepped towards the stern. Allie removed the chains.

"*Iä-R'lyeh!*" the girl cried, so loud it hurt Felix's ears.

"*Cthulhu fhtagn! Iä! Iä!*," the crowd replied.

"It's time," Kimberly repeated, holding her hands out to Felix. He stepped forward and took them.

"Aunt Kimberly, I don't understand," he said.

"You will," she said. "It's my time. I will see you again, in many-columned Y'ha-nthlei, and in that lair of the Deep Ones where we shall dwell amidst wonder and glory forever."

"*Iä-R'lyeh!*" the girl cried again, her voice almost a song.

"*Cthulhu fhtagn! Iä! Iä!*" the crowd replied.

"Open the green gate," Kimberly said to Felix. "Descend the stairs. Learn the truth. Goodbye."

She let go of his hands and turned, then stepped off the boat. Felix rushed to the edge and prepared to dive. Two men in the crowd took his arms, not roughly but with force. Allie rushed to his side.

"She's going home," Allie half-whispered as Felix watched the water, his eyes filling with tears. "And you have much to learn."

The Non-Cult of Unbelieving

When I was fourteen, I had a friend, Bill, who was always running away from home. One time he went camping for a week without telling anyone. Another time he actually joined a carnival, lying about his age. Not quite running away to join the circus, but close. Our senior year of high school he had his best adventure: He joined some kind of cult that was handing out leaflets at the bus station. He told me later that they spent all day begging for money and then had sex parties at night.

Bill was a regular feature in the local paper's "police blotter," as my mother always mentioned, pointedly. "Oh, I see Bill got pulled over for crossing the center line," she might say, looking up from the newspaper. Any such mention would invariably lead her to discuss the cult episode. She had a thing about how stupid cults were. I was in a rebellious phase, so I told her I was going to start my own cult one day. She smiled knowingly and told me I didn't know what I was talking about. That really got me going, so I became a fanatic about cults and religious history in general.

Of course she was right, and when the dust settled, all I had to show for it, other than a deep knowledge of cults, was an enduring dislike not only for cults but for organized religion. Dislike doesn't quite capture it. Abhorrence. I abhor it all.

Cult comes from the French *culte*, in turn from the Latin *cultus*, "care, labor; cultivation, culture; worship, reverence." It was disused after the seventeenth century but revived in the nineteenth with an eye towards distinguishing "cults" from acceptable commonplace "religions," a word which has a direct link to the Latin *religio*, "respect for what is sacred." One hopes for a common root between cult and occult, but unfortunately the latter word comes from the Latin *ob celare*, "to cover over or obscure," while cult is linked to the past participle of *colere*, "to till" (see, also, *colonus, colonia,* the roots of colonist and colony).

Cult's eytmological distinction, like philology itself, is one of effortful degree, an implied excess of labor in reverence that would otherwise be both acceptable and desired. One imagines that the Romans, at least those with republican dispositions or patrician surnames, held excess passion in disdain. Considering the atomic unit of Roman legal thinking, the "citizen," as separate from the whole it underwrites, this makes sense. The dissolution of self that is associated with cultish devotion is anti-subject, anti-citizen.

Cults and religion share a number of features. Can one be a member of a cult while retaining the capacity to act with choice? How many Christian denominations live with a beating cultish heart concealed beneath doctrines of free will? Free to choose but only one choice. There is no strict link between cult and occult, but cult certainly lives there, inside the occult, dragging along the religious who can distinguish their own practice only with deterministic fables dressed up as mysterious puppets.

It is unsurprising that the different strands of early Christians spent a lot of time calling each other insulting names grounded in a scriptural register (see, for example, Elaine Pagel's *The Origins of Satan*). The word cult is just another salvo in the same mudslinging pit.

Now that I've had my fill of cults, I've wanted to fight against them, and fight them with fire by founding my own, but with a decidedly anti-cult bias. That would be a mistake. If I started an anti-cult, there's a distinct possibility I'd just end up with something like a cult, or even worse falling into the kind of jibber jabber libertarians throw around.

My cult will be a non-cult, rooting out the kernel that binds cults to the true foe, the religious. Instead of turtles, a non-cult would have contradictions all the way down, grounded on non-ground, with non-principles and non-members. It should be leaderless with non-mandatory non-rules. You've got to get a hold of the cultish heart firmly and pluck it out and burn it. Better yet, you should chop it up and let it smolder in a golden thurible, swinging from silver chains. Imagine that sweet incense processed down the aisles of a non-church, swirling plumes of smoke around the unbowed heads of the undevoted.

The real problem is how religious thinking inclines people to cultish behavior. It's a good thing to care for other people, but it gets caught up in strange loops when you get devotion to God involved. The trick is you've got to care without caring, dispense with God. It's a question of degree expressed as labor or effort without thinking too hard about it. Mother Theresa spent decades, her faith fled, dressing the wounds of the dying. Her struggle with faith provoked theological handwringing and back-flips to smooth things over. But hostile criticism was equally degraded. The faithful call her a saint. The critics call her a zealous masochist. They both miss the mark. Her non-faith is perhaps her greatest redeeming feature, except its expression in her daily prayer, "Lord I believe, help my unbelief."

Supporters of Saint Theresa reveal their devotional bias to reconcile any ambiguity—they say her belief was primary and her unbelief a weakness for which she sought assistance. Sure, that makes sense. Critics, on the other hand, claim nothing absolves what they argue was substandard care at hospice facilities, including withholding anesthesia, and that her prayer was a false piety.

But what if we take another view, that she hoped God would "help" her unbelief, boost it somehow, and free her from such devotion entirely?

A non-cult knows where the problem lies. When the religiously minded hear Saint Theresa's prayer, they *feel evil*, at a distance but always present. Fear of evil propels them magnetically. Like background radiation, it saturates and excites the world, like ancient mana energy. For them, evil exists, as does their omnipotent, omniscient, omnipresent God. Should God stop evil? Why? Why not? This attracts their attention and energy like no other thing even if they cannot name it, have never thought about it, refuse to acknowledge it. It is, however, the central problem in modern religious thinking, and drives Western thought, even when unannounced. It sits at the table, quietly enjoying its cocktail and that delightful cheese while the other guests argue about banking policy, regressive taxation, the "traditional family," Manifest Destiny, American exceptionalism, and zoning.

Evil is arguably *the* central question in modern thought, but it is too often left in the substrate of discussions on other things, unsatisfactorily resolved while we argue. It has many entertaining solutions. Here's one: God is omnipotent, and evil does exist, but God's very omnipotence means that such evil is both *necessary* and *a moral good*. And pediatric cancer isn't a disease, just one of our "life processes."

Sometimes people try to get at the problem of evil in other ways. You are walking on a bridge over a train junction. There are a main line and a siding. The train is out of control and will crash if not diverted. There are thirty passengers on the train hurtling towards doom. Unfortunately, there is a group of boy scouts hiking on the siding. Ten of them. They will be killed if the train is diverted. Remarkably, on the bridge there is a switching box that will allow you to divert the train, saving the thirty passengers but killing the ten boy scouts. Do you throw the switch?

You are walking through a forest. The path comes to a fork. You go left. Up ahead is a clearing. You enter and see a well. Let's say it is a cute fairytale well, with a little roof over it and a rope on a spindle from which dangles a metal bucket. A child is sitting on the edge. As you approach, the child begins to slip. You lunge forward, diving without any regard for your safety, just catching the back of the child's shirt, hitting your head on the stones, and then falling backwards with the child safely in your arms.

Two different problems. For the first one, I always ask why no one put up fencing to keep people off the siding. Or why doesn't the train have a passive braking system? Did you know that Norwegian nuclear reactors have a passive boron flooding system that completely shuts down any fission activity, without any further human intervention, if it exceeds safe parameters? You'd think that insurers would demand that both fences and passive brakes were part of train operations. I'm not sure why we're getting into arguments about utility, moral choices, etc., when what we should be discussing is poor planning.

For the second one, though, do we say that the act of saving the child by the well is a moral choice? Does the person grabbing the child also "care" about doing so, or is it merely something they do? What if, instead of pulling the child to safety, you pull the shirt away and the child plummets to its death? Or you are just a few more steps away and never get close enough to even touch the child, but dive anyway? Have you done something "good"?

In my proposed non-cult, we care about other people, but we don't care in the sense that we want to make a cult out of what we care about. We dispense with conversion, belief, zealotry, hatred of others. We try to stay calm. We see the world as a child by the well, and concern ourselves with keeping it safe from falling in. Sometimes the child will be too far away, its shirt loose and ill-fitting. Perhaps we will go right and not left, never happening upon that little well with its reckless child perched on the edge. (Reminder: We should educate parents about the dangers posed by unattended wells, encourage proper well fencing, perhaps require all wells to be covered and locked).

A utilitarian sidles up. "Hey, just thought you'd like to read some of our literature on..." No thank you. In a non-cult we don't care about systematizing. Your literature is merely reference material for our discussion with life. Since we don't care, we also don't mind stealing ideas if they are useful, forever seeing them as only ideas. William James put his belief in God down to expedience: When you look at the face of a dead child, does the idea of God help with your grief? I'd say probably.

In a non-cult our indifference is compassionate. It clears the water and the air. We can try now to see each other's face as it is.

A primary concern with cults is orthodoxy. At its root, orthodoxy means "correctness of opinion," usually theological, but it is a lively act of practice. It becomes necessary only when there is a difference of opinion, heterodoxy. Behind all this is doxa, which means "To appear, to seem, to think, to accept." Doxa is used in the Septuagint, a Greek translation of the Hebrew Old Testament, as the word to replace "kavod," Hebrew for "glory." This conjures a sense of immanence, things manifesting in and of themselves, a self-evident revelation of the divine. It should be incontrovertible, but then suddenly it isn't. Hence, orthodoxy creeps into the mix.

You can imagine what the non-cult of unbelieving has to say about all that. First, call it what it is: You are all arguing about what people believe as an excuse to boss everybody around. Take the color red. I hold up a sheet of red paper and say, "This is red paper." You nod in agreement. We verify the wavelength and frequency of the light. But what does it *mean* to see red? We could study all sorts of psychological effects, poetic references, artistic achievements, its impact on productivity, taste, hair loss, even consider whether cats and dogs prefer red collars, and we haven't nailed down what red does in our heads. Everything else is secondary and subsidiary to the revelation, the redness, which we lose sight of.

If you're talking about the truth, especially divine truth, you've already left it far behind. No amount of chalk, no length of string, no trail of breadcrumbs is going to lead you out of the maze of orthodoxy. You're already telling a joke and explaining why it's funny at the same time and no one is going to laugh. Not at the joke, anyway.

That's the non-cult's true power, its most tangential and thus central unbelief: We don't have any. That's the axis on which it all turns. And despite anything more I could say about other cults or religions, in the end it is, or would be, its fatal flaw.

I once saw a film about a Buddhist monk's life. It was a biography of sorts, a slow film in terms of action but a deep study of his spiritual path through life. In the end, it was the story of how a young monk prepares to become an old monk, one who faces not just the challenges of life but the reality of death. The more I've thought about it, the more it makes my dream of the non-cult of unbelieving strong.

My teenage, angst-inflected study of cults found a lot of weird stuff. A lot. But there was one account that always stood out. It inspired my quixotic dream of founding the non-cult of unbelieving, even if it signaled the inevitability of failure. Listen, then, to the story of the Marrow Islanders and their tragic fate, drawn from their own accounts.

In 1938, a group of seven disillusioned Oblates of Mary Magdalene left the order, frustrated by abuse and neglect at the residential school where they worked. They moved to Marrow Island off the New Brunswick coast near Shippagan. There is a small but sheltered cove on the western side, protected from the rolling Atlantic swells by a ridge. Fish are plentiful, the land rugged but fertile, and while winters are dark and long, summer is a time of abundance.

The settlers built a large white clapboard bunkhouse and kitchen and a chapel from stones they found on the island. Their leader of sorts, Agnar Hansen, was a Norwegian and former electrical engineer who fled before the Nazi occupation. He decided they should build a sauna. He also used their last bit of savings to purchase a boat, and the group fished for cod and other things, salting it for sale. They lived quietly and peacefully for several years.

With their departure from the oblates, the group had also left the Roman Catholic Church, and they only used the chapel for silent prayer with no directed services. They all had and read bibles, shared ideas and discussed their thoughts and feelings, but there was no pretense of organized religion. They worked, ate, and lived together, motivated by their experience of injustice and hopes for the future.

Agnar, however, stopped praying in the chapel, choosing instead to climb the ridge and look to the east at sunrise each day. He built a hermitage at the ridge top with stones and driftwood and began to sleep there by himself. Gradually, the others stopped praying, too, and occupied with the work of fishing and salting or cultivating vegetables, the already faint echoes of their religious lives dropped away, replaced with the deep satisfaction of their connection to the material world.

"We were living day to day, but with a sense of community," wrote one. "It was as if we could hear the rhythm of life and the seasons."

They had all been celibate (they divided the bunkhouse into private rooms), but two pairs decided to get married, build small homes, and raise families. They agreed to keep the communal kitchen, raise any children collectively, and continue to share their resources. Agnar, now silently participating in work and retreating to his hermitage, said nothing. In addition to staring out at the sunrise each morning, he would end his day staring at the sunset.

One night, during a windstorm, one of the group went to check on the small flock of sheep they had recently added to their operations. As she ascended the ridge, she saw Agnar walk out of his hermitage to look east over the water. Following, she watched him stand on a small promontory as the moon rose, then after a few minutes return to the hut.

"Agnar is watching the moon rise now," she told the others.

"It's a beautiful thing to see," said another.

"Does he watch it set, too?" someone asked.

"That's not really that interesting," someone said. "Is it?"

None of them had ever really thought about moon set, though they knew the moon rose in the east and set in the west, and that the times and points of rising and setting varied over the year. In the end they all decided to look it up in the almanac and then see if Agnar was watching the moon set as well as the sunrise, sunset, and moon rise.

He was. At 2:40 AM, he walked down to the cove and stood on the jetty as the moon set.

A few weeks later, when the others were out fishing, one couple stayed behind to tend the sheep and garden. One went over to the east side looking for the flock and passed by Agnar's hut. Surrounding it were small cairns in a regular pattern that reminded him of Stonehenge. Angar had painted the walls with something rusty in color and also strung garlands of woven seaweed along the eaves of the little thatched roof.

Eventually, the group decided to ask Agnar what was up. After some polite questions about health and a discussion of the new winch for the boat, Mina, a likable, no-nonsense Québécois from Trois-Rivieres, got to it.

"What's going on, Agnar?" she said. "You've been a little withdrawn lately. And always up with the sun, watching the sunset, the moon. Now the stones, and whatever you've done with the hermitage."

Agnar sat silently.

"We just want to know that you are all right."

Agnar turned his head to one side, narrowed his eyes, and nodded. It was hard to tell what that meant.

"Is something going on with you?" Mina asked.

Agnar considered this, still nodding. After a brief pause, he spoke.

"We'll see," he said, then stood and walked up the ridge.

Agnar kept to his schedule of sun and moon watching, fished most days, and said nothing.

As the autumnal equinox approached, the group spent most of a week in the big kitchen canning tomatoes, squash, and other vegetables. Agnar had taken to muttering over the jars as they sat in the water bath. He also asked politely if he could slaughter the chickens for Sunday dinner, which seemed like he was reconnecting with the group in some way. He even offered a silent grace before the meal, standing as he used to do at the head of the table. And while he didn't talk at the meal, he did seem to listen and even laughed once or twice, thoughtfully chewing a crust of bread.

The night of the equinox was uncommonly still for Marrow Island, and the sky a clear pane of glass against the starlit infinity of heaven. A full moon rose, its spectral light crisp in the cooling air. Despite reservations, the group had decided to "keep an eye" on Agnar, which meant someone checked on him discretely at sunrise, sunset, and so on.

As Mina approached the top of the ridge, she saw Agnar, presumably out to watch the moon rise. Getter closer, though, she could see he was naked. His entire body glistened darkly, his eyes floating brightly in the black oval of his face. Suddenly, he turned towards her, running as fast as he could. He was yelling—almost barking—and since he was barefoot his stride was erratic, a side to side hopping over the rocky terrain. Mina turned and ran down, shouting for help.

Everyone straggled out into the yard by the kitchen, looking up at the ridge. Mina was well ahead of Agnar, who stopped about halfway down. His barking reached a crescendo in a howl, followed by heavy panting as he stood, head down, and began to sob. In the thin light they could see he was covered in blood, presumably from the chickens he'd slaughtered earlier. He turned and walked back up the ridge.

Seized by a mixture of fear and alarm, the group went after him.

When they reached the top, the moonlight was bright enough for them to see Agnar with his back to them, out on the thin tail of the ridge that ended in a promontory over the ocean. His hands were raised, in one of them a knife. He then brought the knife down out of view, working it with both hands at something below his midsection. After a few seconds, he raised his hands again, one with the knife and the other with a shapeless clump. Then he simply tipped forward over the edge.

The group rushed to the promontory, carefully looking over the edge, but Agnar was gone.

After inspecting Agnar's hut and the shrine he had built to the sun and moon and whatever else whispered to him, the group decided to leave Marrow Island. On the last trip shuttling their belongings and livestock to shore, someone said to Mina, in a sad, reserved way, "What was he thinking?"

Mina cast her gaze down and then, brushing the hair from her face, said, "What you mean is 'What did he believe?'"

Before My Ritual Suicide

I woke up early, too early for a ritual suicide, but it was a cool and windy morning in June, and I fell back asleep for several hours, which was delightful. Just outside my window, in one of the verdant box elder trees I had pruned back hard last summer, robins built a nest last month. Three large birds pranced on the lawn beneath in a belligerent avian display.

I drove into town for a cup of coffee, an indulgent distraction from the day's events. On the way, I passed the elementary school. It's named after Russell Newbury, a botanist who worked on hybrid grains, notably rice, in the 1950s. I attended Newbury for six years. Since it is June, the school was abandoned, so I decided to take a walk and see the old playground.

The first person I knew who died was named Abby. I don't remember her last name. I was in first grade, and our classroom was at the back of the building at ground level, functionally an extension to the boiler room. In winter, it was always warm and cozy, and it felt separate from the rest of the school, except on trips to the gymnasium or at lunch. And recess. The playground was right outside, and the classroom had its own door opening right on to it.

It was the spring of 1971. First graders had recess twice a day. The other classrooms were on the first floor, but since that part of the building was on a hill these were also at ground level. The playground sat at the bottom of the hill, with a long slope leading up to these other classrooms, and at the start of recess the other children would stream out and run down the hill to where my class was already waiting.

The playground had the usual: An exceptionally low basketball hoop, see-saws, a merry-go-round, metal slides, and a jungle gym dreamed up by an orthopedist, a lethal arrangement of metal pipes. As always with children, we played on and, more importantly, around all this. There was a flowing drama and fantasy of intrigue, gossip, and

75

the first pretensions to flirting and friendship connecting the different activities by whispers, finger pointing, and couriers running from group to group. I imagine Machiavelli standing on the steps of the Duomo di Firenze watching the children scamper to and fro, thinking "Is it better to be hated or feared?"

Abby was not in my class, and I only knew her in the way that you know children not in your class, by way of rumor. And she had disappeared. This disappearance was notable in that even the parents and teachers were both aware of it and whispering about it themselves, some even mentioning it to their own children with explanations and injunctions "to be nice to Abby." This mystery floated over us for weeks, until one day Abby returned, and with her return the injunction was repeated with the added force of "don't let me catch you teasing that girl."

I was standing on the hill with friends. I can't recall whatever hijinks we were up to. I know that there were two or three precocious girls who were demanding to know which of them various popular boys liked. Such allegiances were entirely new to me. The whistle blew, telling us it was time to line up and return to class.

As a general matter, the lining up process was chaotic. It caught children off guard, in the middle of a game or about to have a turn on the slide, any activity that they preferred over class, and especially in pleasant weather. Afternoon recess was usually worse, as it was that day, because the prospect of returning to class with only a brief time before the tantalizing prospect of dismissal made schoolwork even more tedious. Even now, the ways schoolwork was tedious is such a distracting topic it makes me want to abandon everything and just run around in sneakers.

I made it to my line, all of us grudgingly facing the teacher on duty, her arms folded impatiently. Suddenly, far down the lines, there was a commotion. The lines broke up in the uproar, children backing away, running, yelling. The crowd was loose enough so I could see the teacher rushing forward and grabbing a boy roughly by the arm. A few feet away, Abby stood alone, clutching her bald head. The boy had her wig in his hands. My teacher, Mrs. Rimmer, ran from our classroom, and another teacher came out of one of the portable classrooms next to the playground.

Before 1968, pediatric doctors considered leukemia an incurable disease. Today, sixty-seven years later, the survival rate is roughly 85%. This remarkable achievement was driven by Donald Pinkel at St. Jude's Hospital, and an approach he called Total Therapy. Total Therapy involved multiple cancer suppressing doses at their highest dose, radiation, and years-long chemotherapy. By 1970, St. Jude's had a documented survival rate of 50%. Individually, the treatments weren't experimental, but the intensity of the regimen was new.

Leukemia comes from Greek, meaning "white blood," so named for the waves of immature white blood cells, lymphoblasts, the cancer unleashes. Since it is blood borne, it attacks the entire body, crowding out healthy blood cells for lymphoblasts that then attack organs. Early monotherapies worked seriatim, using one then another in hopes of finding the key to suppressing the disease. Pinkel abandoned it as futile, since at best it extended the life of a child for a few months but never offered a cure. Total Therapy was a go-for-broke try for a cure. And it worked for some, an achievement already almost miraculous.

Total Therapy's broad spectrum, high intensity approach had side-effects, notably hair loss. Abby had returned to school after treatment for an otherwise fatal disease, using an experimental method that had roughly a 50% chance of working, having lost her hair and wearing a wig. And a boy yanked it off her head as the entire first grade was lining up at the end of recess. She was seven years old.

She never returned to school and died three months later.

I walked around the playground for a few minutes. All the equipment has been replaced with the brightly colored and decidedly safer variety made from recycled plastics and set out on beds of shredded rubber. They have added an amphitheater cut into the hill, with neat rows and a circular stage fashioned from cement. In the middle of the stage is a puppet theater that was a gift from a sister school in Japan. I stood behind it and pretended to put on a puppet show with my hands as puppets. I don't know any of the usual puppet stories well enough, like Punch and Judy, so I did one I called "Abby's Wig."

It started to rain, so I got back in the car and drove to the hardware store. In my pocket was a list of things I needed scrawled on the back of an envelope from the outfit that manages my retirement account: Rope, wire, mousetraps, heavy duty plastic sheeting.

Along the side of the building there is a lean-to with rental equipment underneath it, things like gas-powered tillers, log splitters, lawn rollers, even an aerator you can tow behind a lawn tractor. Lawn aeration is important, but I don't know anyone who actually does it regularly. Just mowing a lawn and the action of rainfall can lead to thatch, the accumulation of material that compacts and takes a long time to decompose. Aerators pull little plugs out of the soil and make room for nutrients, water, and new growth. You basically rip up your lawn a little, like hair plugs that don't get replaced, and then the lawn can grow. A metaphor.

The rope is inside, along the back wall. It's stored on rolls suspended on a rack. They have natural ropes, like jute and cotton, and all kinds of synthetic ones. I was surprised to see old fashioned clothesline made from plastic covered wire, but I went with the more traditional jute, fifteen feet of it.

It was only mid-morning, but I was hungry and stopped by the diner next to the Blue Chalet Motel. It was mostly empty, but there were two tourists at the counter asking Allison about the strawberry festival, which isn't for another month.

"They've got the family festival this Saturday," Allison said. "It's a lot of fun."

"What's the theme?" asked one of the tourists.

"Well, family, I suppose," Allison said, pouring coffee and putting it in front of me. "The Life Church puts it on. Maybe you saw their billboard on the way into town."

They hadn't.

"It's the one with the pledge of allegiance on it. Part of it, at least."

The diner has good coffee, and I ordered cherry pie to go with it.

On the way back to the house, I stopped by the Methodist church I attend. There is a large extension at the back with a meeting room named after Booker Ferguson, who wrote a book about Methodist history in America. He lived in town during the 1970s and contributed to Reader's Digest regularly. Ferguson was a sprightly little man, with white hair and a florid expression, and a bright smile. He wore horn-rimmed glasses. He looked like Colonel Sander's cheerfully intellectual brother.

Between Ferguson Hall and the sanctuary is a hallway with classrooms for Sunday school. At the end of the hallway is a wall with paneling that conceals a circular stairway up to the pulpit. After services and class, there's a coffee in Ferguson Hall, but the children sneak up the hidden stairs and run around behind the pulpit, crawling behind the organ's pipe screen or scurrying up the stairs to the choir balcony. They are always quiet, never speaking above a whisper. The lights are off, but the afternoon sun filters through the stained-glass windows in an antique shaded yellow glow, like lacquer on an old painting. There are twelve windows, one for each apostle, depicting a defining scene for each from the gospel, except for Bartholomew, who stands next to Christ with his left hand on his bared chest and his right hand extended, holding a curved knife.

When I was a child, I memorized the names of the books of the bible to please my Sunday school teacher, Mrs. Powell. Once, after class, we all walked under the stained-glass windows, Mrs. Powell quizzing us about each apostle and the event depicted. Simon with his fishing nets.

Andrew and his loaves and fishes. Judas and his kiss. And Bartholomew with his knife.

Mr. Ferguson was invited to speak to our class from time to time, and he was the first adult I knew, besides Mrs. Powell, who knew how to talk about religion to children without making it sound like a fantasy. Even the pastor, Reverend Booth, tended to blur the lines around things. Mr. Ferguson presented things directly, with a simplicity that held the essential of a thing. One time he talked to us about the devil, without mincing words.

"He's the enemy," Mr. Ferguson said. "Think about all the good things we have. A family, a home, food to eat. The devil doesn't want you to have those. Even worse, the devil doesn't want love. He hates it. Love and kindness are the things the devil wants to take away from you."

I raised my hand, and he nodded at me, smiling.

"What should we do?" I asked.

"Pray," he said. "Come to church on Sunday. Listen to your parents and the pastor. Pay attention in class. And whenever you can, resist evil things."

We were all sitting cross-legged in a circle. Mr. Ferguson was sitting on a little wooden chair. Usually, adults looked funny in the classroom, because all the furniture was little, but Mr. Ferguson didn't. He was short but also quite slenderly built, with fine hands and clothes that seemed slightly too big.

"It's a matter of habits," he said. "One has to organize to beat the devil. Faith and love are habits."

There is an old disused graveyard next to the church, beneath overgrown pine trees. A fish merchant from one town over once received a shipment with a spoiled swordfish, and buried it there, clandestinely, in a shallow hole. It took a week for the caretaker to notice the smell and find the patch of turned earth. There followed a brief interval of mystery, until the head of the church council, a no-nonsense man who owned the local grocery, took a shovel and dug it up, loaded it in a truck, and threw it on the sidewalk in front of the culprit's store. My mother continued to shop there. The floor was covered with sawdust and there were crates of Portuguese salt cod piled by the door.

My grandfather is buried in the graveyard. At his burial, the pastor read the funeral service and some notes, fumbling a few of the family names and giving a general but incomplete sense of the man. Then the masons came forward, draped a white leather apron on a small stool by the casket, and placed a sprig of acacia on top. A somber man with neat hair in a black suit, wearing a blue and white apron and a necklace with square and compass, stepped forward, raising his white-gloved hands. He produced a roll of paper and read my grandfather's name, noted he was a 32nd degree mason, and listed his achievements as the county engineer. Placing the roll next to the acacia, he turned towards the mourners.

"We celebrate his life," he said, outstretched palms facing down. The other masons did likewise.

"We cherish his memory in our hearts," he said, crossing his hands over his chest.

"We commend his spirit to God, who gave it," he said, raising his hands. "The Lord said to Moses, 'Tell Aaron and his sons, this is how you are to bless the Israelites. Say to them: The Lord bless you and keep you; The Lord make his face shine on you and be gracious to you; The Lord turn his face toward you and give you peace. So they will put my name on the Israelites, and I will bless them.'"

After a moment, he collected the roll and acacia from the stool. Two of the other masons neatly folded the apron, like it was the flag.

I walked out the back of the graveyard into the forest. There's a path that slopes upwards. After a five minutes' walk, you come to an old greenhouse, its metal frame rusted and its roof a patchwork of cracked or missing panes. A little further on is an abandoned swimming pool, the bottom filled with dead leaves and water the color of dirt. Beyond a row of untidy hedges is the abandoned Dickinson place, a mansion that's collapsing brick by brick into a heap of forgotten memories.

When I was twelve, we'd ride our bikes there and pick through the junk inside. I found a trunk filled with newspapers from the 1940s, with headlines about the war and FDR and rationing. My friend, Richard, found a scuttle filled with anthracite coal, glistening and sharp like glass, and we took a piece to his house and burnt it in the fireplace, just to see what it was like. With the chimney cold, the smoke billowed out, and the living room smelled like burnt matches. From the kitchen, Richard's mother asked us what the hell we were doing. Richard told her.

"Boys," she said, walking into the room, "don't go to the Dickinson place. You know that. It's dangerous. Oh, God, open a window."

"Who were the Dickinsons, anyway," Richard asked, poking the coal to the back of the fireplace.

"Open a window, Richard," she said. "They were crazy rich people."

"What happened to them?" Richard asked.

"I don't know," she said, looking into the fireplace. "They had big parties, with lots of cars. People drove up from the city. It was a long time ago, when I was a child. My mother said old man Dickinson made a fortune as a bootlegger, then got into high fashion. His wife was model for Vogue magazine. She was southern, very elegant."

"But what happened?" Richard said.

"She shot him," she said. "Then she killed herself. God, that smell is awful. Go open a window, Richard, then wash your hands. If you're staying for dinner Mark, call your mother."

The drive back home from the church was uneventful, but at least now I've got everything I need. It's funny the things you remember at a time like this. When my wife was alive, she would listen to me talk about this town, the places and people, the memories, and say "That's why I don't like maps. They don't have the important stuff."

I Got Some Brain Damage

My father taught me to make my bed first thing, right after I got up, "before it slipped my mind." That was good advice. If you keep the world around you orderly, it improves the quality of your mind and spirit. Years later I realized "before it slipped my mind" should be "before it slipped *from* my mind." The "from" was missing. The "it" was not "making my bed," but rather the unmade bed, just as I had left it, slept in and dream-tossed, threatening to "slip" my mind in its dream-tossed shape. Yes, nothing threatens to slip one's mind like those crumpled sheets and blankets, slick as they are with nocturnal confusion.

People wonder how I ended up in a psychiatric hospital.

I got some brain damage. You can probably tell. It wasn't all at once, for which I am thankful. There were the concussions as a child, something like ten of them, and then the martial arts when I was twelve, which is a lot of fun despite the blows to the head. Then there was the accident. Technically it did not damage my brain, but by damaging pretty much everything else except my legs it made the existing damage worse somehow.

Strange, then, that with so much brain damage I've been able to "function at a high level," as Dr. Ogilvy says. I find it strange when people think that brain damage isn't exactly what's required for high level function. Everyone functions pretty much like everyone else, unless they have brain damage, so who is to say that it's good or bad. Maybe just a certain kind of brain damage is good. I don't know. I've noticed that many people without any apparent brain damage function in what I would term a low level, indifferent to the suffering of others and themselves. I ask myself that all the time. How do my actions or failures to act affect those around me and elsewhere? Apparently, that's the root of all my psychological problems, although I see those problems as distinct from all the brain damage. Then, of course, there was the accident.

I say, "the accident," but it was largely my own fault. In 1994, I burned down Rolling Pin Bowling Alley the day after Thanksgiving. Not everyone goes shopping that day, Black Friday, which I didn't know. I thought a bowling alley would be empty. My parents were both psychologists. That's not an explanation or justification, but growing up I did hear a lot about "the pernicious effects of consumer society" and impulse buying, stuff like that. Anyway, it wasn't much of a bowling alley, mostly just kids dropped off for birthday parties, maybe a geriatric bowling league on weeknights. And I thought the bowling alley would be empty, or close to empty. It was Black Friday.

I also didn't know that the warehouse next door was full of magnesium, or that it shared a sprinkler system with the bowling alley. When the whole thing exploded, I was more surprised than anyone. I was fourteen and had only the roughest, 1994 United States public education ideas about chemistry, so you can imagine my surprise when a routine fire at a bowling alley detonated, destroying four blocks, including a paint store, a presbyterian church, and a Ford dealership. That magnesium was improperly stored is all I'm saying. Really, it was.

That's a long way of saying that I wasn't trying to kill anyone, or at least not as many people as I did kill. Of course, I knew there were risks. You don't set fire to a bowling alley without knowing, at least somewhere deep inside, that something bad could happen. I had seen a man die the summer before, in the parking lot at the beach, and it scared the hell out of me. He was an older man with a pot belly in a bathing suit and flip flops, a towel flung over his shoulder, standing by a blue Chrysler station wagon. Suddenly, he made a choking sound, clutched his chest, and fell flat on his face, turning blue. Someone tried CPR, but when the paramedics arrived, they just covered him up and carted him off. It reminded me of Wallace Stevens and that poem about the rooster in the woods. Like, what if Wallace Stevens was walking to the beach with a towel over his shoulder and died from a heart attack. The guy looked like that. After that, death had a grim reality for me that only deepened after the bowling alley fiasco.

So, yes, I am in a mental hospital of a *type*. At first it was a juvenile forensic psychiatric hospital named Gracefield. In 1998, I was reevaluated, determined to still be unstable, and sent to an adult version of the same thing, which was something of an improvement, but not much. This hospital is called Blackmoor.

Here's what I do all day: eat, sit around a day room and write (everyone else plays cards or watches television), go outside for an hour and walk around and around and around, go to group. Group is group therapy and is pretty much what you think it is. Once a week I see a psychiatrist, usually Dr. Ogilvy, who isn't British, but I act like he is.

I've only seen it once, but from the front the building is surprisingly nondescript, a four-story number with thin windows and a facade that looks like someone glued rocks to it. There are three flag poles and lots of shrubberies they've let go. It looks like a high school in a made for TV movie about teenagers experimenting with drugs, which isn't far from the truth. There is a circle of asphalt right in front to turn around in after the van dumps you here. No other patient I know has ever left, except when they died, and I'm not so sure even then.

The idea is simple. People who are patients here committed criminal acts, but they were determined to be mentally ill such that they cannot be held responsible for those actions. I've got schizoaffective disorder, which is basically schizophrenia with depression mixed in, and this is where Dr. Ogilvy thinks my brain damage is to blame, but he can't say for sure. I take Euphodiperidone and some other pill, which I think is to counteract the side-effects of Euphodiperidone, but I'm not sure. Other patients complain about Euphodiperidone, but other than tremors and sexual dysfunction and sometimes forgetting where I am, no complaints from me. There's this one guy, Gerald, and it made him incontinent—I mean completely and in every way—so now he wears diapers. Looking good, Gerald!

A subset of patients are passing through, and they don't count. They're getting evaluations before trial, things like that, and don't mix with our kind. We're not mean to them, but it's the same thing as not naming farm animals.

I know everyone, but I'm only friendly with a few. My roommate, Vivian, doesn't speak and I have no idea why he's here instead of prison. He strangled his grandmother. Leonard drove a school bus for twenty years, then one day ran into a bank naked holding a shotgun. Roberto burned his house down with his wife and children locked inside. Jojo (not his real name) tried but failed (I think it makes a difference) to shoot up a congregation of Jehovah's witnesses. A man named Art Burbank, one of the elders, was at the door and somehow convinced Jojo to stop. Jojo says Art gave him a copy of The Watch Tower with a picture of a bear, a lion, and a lamb lying in a blueberry patch together, and there was another picture with a Japanese family in kimonos who were living in the eternity of God's future paradise.

There are others: Grant drowned his wife; Sam put a gun to a grocery clerk's head; Arthur drove his car into a shopping mall; Ned beat up his wife and daughter.

It's all terrible, and it's terrible to live with the memories. That's the difference. None of us would do those things now, not with Euphodiperidone coursing through our veins and breakfast then the day room and then going outside and walking around and around and then group. And, of course, seeing a psychiatrist once a week.

Dr. Ogilvy is in charge, a corpulent man of choleric temper, yet always kind to us, the patients. There are usually two other doctors, but they only stay for a year or so. Presumably, they're studying us and psychiatry, since they're much younger and don't talk nearly as much as Dr. Ogilvy. There are two therapists who lead group, and that's really where the action is. One is Brenda, the smart one. She used to be married to a diplomat from Senegal and still visits him, which I think is nice. There's a picture of Yossou N'Dour in her office, and she plays his music all the time. The other therapist is Jerry, not that smart but never gets mad at anyone, which I also think is nice.

When we see Dr. Ogilvy, the other doctors sit on either side taking notes and asking a lot of questions. If it's something personal, I usually answer, but Dr. Ogilvy answers for me sometimes.

"How are you feeling today?" a doctor might say.

"Good," I say. "Very good. I went for a walk."

"Do you ever hear things that other people cannot hear?" the other doctor might ask.

"Michael hasn't had hallucinations for several years," Dr. Ogilvy says. I have no idea if that's true, but if Dr. Ogilvy says so I'm okay with it.

"So, no whispering or voices?" the first doctor says.

"You're much better, aren't you Michael?" Dr. Ogilvy says.

"Yes," I say, although I'm not sure. I mean, I burned down a bowling alley. And then there was the explosion.

That's why group is where the action is. The Brenda and Jerry show, I call it. Brenda keeps things going and Jerry is right there for you. We get in a circle, and each of us gets to talk about whatever. And I mean whatever. Leonard once talked about barbecue for like an hour, how much he missed going to barbecues, what they ate, who was there, everything. You could tell Brenda was pleased. At the end, when he started crying and the subject of Jesus came up, Jerry went over and gave Leonard a hug. It was great.

There's other staff. The important ones are nurses, since they keep the day going. We just call them "nurse." The other ones are probably "orderlies," but we don't call them "orderlies," because that seems rude. We are all on a first name basis. There's Joe, Linda, Mike, and George. Contrary to what you may have seen in the cinema, they do not torture or harass us, since that's what most of us do to ourselves and more effectively than they ever could.

All this probably seems quite normal, I'm sure, but it's not. Take mealtime, for instance. We line up in the hallway and wait. And wait. And wait. There's a lot of waiting. When the door opens, Linda is there, and the food is already on plates at the counter. No forks or knives, only spoons, and they count those up at the end. Usually no one talks during mealtime. I have no idea why. It's weird.

The day room is also weird. Everyone wears these pajamas-like things all the time, so there's that. Since we only have one television, people fight over what to watch. And you have to be there. Not like "Oh, you *have* to be there," they lock us in. The good thing is that the television brings the rest of world to us, so I know who Taylor Swift is, things like that. I would rather be in my room, since most of the time I'm writing, but the television is an important link to the ebbs and flows of what is happening in the outside the world, although it is filtered and manipulated into television fantasy. It would be an interesting project to interview us and figure out how television has warped our perception of reality, and I think we'd be willing subjects, at least Vivian, Leonard, Roberto, Jojo, and I. Most of us sufficiently distort reality that it might offset or neutralize anything the television people do. For example, if you asked Roberto about The Brady Bunch or Two Broke Girls (his favorite), I bet he'd tell you about the impact of family dynamics on adolescent development or contrasts in worldviews based on wealth. Criminally insane people watching daytime television absorbing all that broadcast fantasy and processing it back, through layers of madness, into something accurate and true. There's graduate thesis greatness waiting, for sure.

Speaking of distortions, I don't want to leave the impression that life in a forensic psychiatric hospital is as nice as it sounds. Good medical care, meals, group, and friends. Pretty nice, but there are obvious downsides. We're locked in here, but that doesn't bother most of us as much as you'd think. Also, when people have bad days, they have *bad* days, while there is a definite ceiling to good days. And there are locks. I don't mean the main doors. Bedrooms, offices, the day room: All locked. Interior movement is restricted, a kind of crowd control that follows the cycle of the day as patients pass from bedrooms to dining room to day room to group, doors locking behind as we move. The day ends, meds are passed, and the final locked door closes. The symbol of my life, the "snick" of a lock bolt.

That is until recently. I have calendrical anxiety, so keeping track of minutes, hours, days, weeks, and months is a problem, but my best guess would be six months ago. I was in bed watching the glow of the ancient sodium light outside my window, and I heard the lock go snick. It was the middle of the night. Something was truly amiss, I thought, perhaps an emergency, surely an accident of some kind. Vivian, one of the more heavily medicated among us, slept on, and if there was a required evacuation it was up to me to investigate.

I tested the handle, found it unlocked, and opened door. The hallway was dark except for the reassuring night lights at regular intervals, which give the bland institutional hallway a disarmingly charming appearance, like the lobby of theater. I listened but heard nothing at first, and then came a tapping, someone walking quickly or even running, away from the nurse's station and back into the older part of the building. As far as I know, it is disused, and has been for some time, ever since President Reagan pushed the repeal of the Mental Health Systems Act of 1980. But, as the footsteps receded, I heard a door open then close. Another lock snicked, and it was quiet again. I returned to bed but did not sleep for hours. When morning came, our door was locked again.

The next night, I was awake but had my eyes closed, watching the pattern across the inside of my eyelids, when the lock snicked again. Quickly this time, I opened the door and padded quietly in the direction the steps had fled before, coming eventually to the double doors at the end of the hallway. These were always locked and unused, but when I pushed the bar, the door popped open and I heard the footsteps again.

Despite my confinement, I do not long for escape and freedom, so when I passed through the door into the older section of the hospital it was curiosity and the intrigue of whatever mystery was unfolding that drove me. The hallway here was dark, but a row of high windows admitted light from outside, and I could see in half shadow a stray wheelchair, several half-opened doors, and a pile of boxes filled with files and papers. Then, the footsteps again, louder but light, as if made by small feet going quickly, at the far end where darkness was still complete. I followed them, hands out in caution, and stumbled over a pile of clothing or towels, regained my feet, and wandered on until the hallway turned. There were stairs and a dim light at the bottom, so I pressed on, coming to an open door. Inside was a wooden bench, like in a locker room, and the floor was tiled, and to the right, just visible in the light coming in the door, were showers, the kind that stand in columns with several shower heads on each.

Out from behind the showers stepped a figure. At first, I thought it was a boy. He had on a blue uniform, like a cub scout, and moved his arms and legs clumsily. As he stepped closer, I could see his face and arms were glossy, as if they were plastic or painted wood. His expression was oddly blank, and he turned his head side to side as he teetered forward. Another one appeared, then another, all dressed the same. Then two girls stepped out, one with braids and both wearing tights and sweaters. They came past the showers then stopped abruptly, standing completely still.

I was both aghast at their shiny faces and skin and mystified by their jerky little movements, but standing still they seemed nothing more than puppets without strings.

"Who are you?" I said, my voice loud against the tiled floor and walls. At this, they turned their heads mechanically to look at one another, their little cylindrical heads going side to side, but stopped after a moment and stared back at me.

I backed away, and they followed, arms pumping up and down as they walked on their stiff little legs in quick, small steps. They were not fast, at least not very fast, and I turned and ran away, not stopping until I reached my room and closed the door behind me.

You would think that a troop of doll children in a hospital shower could not go undiscovered, but there they were. My hallucinations, when I had them, paled next to these creatures. At most I had a buzz of lightly whispering voices, and these did nothing more than comment on my thoughts in generally uncomplimentary ways. The doll children were detailed and distinct, their strange defects rendered so consistently—the round heads, the shiny skin, the beady eyes—that I concluded they were both real and a separate species.

Weeks passed (I think) until my bedroom door again unlocked. This time, I resolved to go directly to the shower room. There, the doll children had already lined up, tallest to shortest, facing the door. Unsure what to do, I took a seat on the bench and waited. At once, the doll children began to move, lifting their legs and putting them down, then swinging their arms, bowing at intervals, all out of sync but in the same pattern. The clicking of their hard little feet on the tile floor came in and out of rhythm, sometimes just a clattering jumble, but then for a moment in uniform cadence.

Then they stopped in a rackety jumble, one after another. On impulse, I began to clap, but they just stood there in a line, unblinking. After a few minutes, I left.

These "performances" continued sporadically for weeks, each one with better timing and coordination. Why would doll children puppets be here, in the disused wing of a forensic psychiatric hospital, incubating, practicing their dance? And why for me? I thought about telling Brenda and the group, but then Dr. Ogilvy would get involved, and I'd be taking something a lot stronger than Euphodiperidone. The prospect of joining George in the diaper club was ominous, so I said nothing.

Then came the final performance of the doll children puppets in the shower room. I say "final," but what I mean is the other performances were clearly rehearsal. This was the first true performance, polished and skilled.

I knew it was show time right away. The showers were decorated with a "Happy Birthday" sign, and a small table with a cake and candles was in the center of the "stage." The doll children marched in and began their dance, now well-rehearsed, clacking their tiny dance and pantomime. Finally, I saw what the stiff little arms meant by swinging, what the feet communicated in their unbalanced shuffle, and I was reminded of an obvious fact that one forgets in the busy rush of life. People are born every day, even the day after Thanksgiving.

I go to see their show every few nights now. They have started to speak or sing, I'm not sure which. It might be that they are screaming. The show always stops before the explosion, though, and I'm thankful for that.

The Unpeopled Island in the River

The unpeopled island sat to the east of town in an incised meander of the river that flowed around it. To the north and south of the island, sandbars shifted in the wider stretches of the river with the seasons of flood. Strips of standing grass on their uncertain banks bent in the wind. In summer, boats of day trippers visited the sandbars' sun-drenched, slanted beaches. These were treacherous. River currents often cut underneath, leeching out their tenuous support, and a wrong step might send you through the hollow shell of sand into the swift current beneath. A man once saw his wife and two children disappear when a black hole opened below them, followed by chunks of wet sand breaking off and dissolving in the currents. The unfortunate victims were drawn down, under the length of the sandbar, then released into the flow at uncertain depths. The bodies never came up.

The island, though, never moved. It was fixed in its narrow curve, with a massive rock outcropping surrounded by trees that anchored the whole affair to the riverbed. The shoreline, too, was all rock.

The island was much longer than its width, with a point at each tip, like a knife wound in the riverbed had let the rocky crust of earth erupt and freeze, preserved against both the spring flood and the chopping abrasions of rafting ice. Stands of mulberry and beech trees crowded the island, thick and untended, with a tight mass of low branches that harassed visitors. Their berries and beechnuts, though, sustained a rookery in spring and summer. There was a rafter of aggressive turkeys that slept in the branches of a dead tree lurking in the shadow of the outcropping.

Despite its constant nature, the island was unpeopled. It was fairly large, more than half a mile in length, but the town had instead grown on the western bank, which followed the smaller of the river channels that surrounded the island. A short bridge could have reached it easily, even though the river ran deepest there. Trees could have been cut, ground leveled, pipelines run from the shore for water and gas, and yet they never were. The idea never entered anyone's mind.

At first, it was the simple practicality of more accessible land. The town sat on a flat stretch next to the river that backed up on a ridge. That is where downtown started, with a stop for the river boat, a general store, and a quaint boarding house, the first steady markers of frontier settlement. A grid of streets and a set of respectable homes came next, then a church, a school, and a building with offices for a lawyer, doctor, and accountant. The courthouse and cemetery came next, followed by their intermediary, the jail. The town lay claim to the mantle of civilization.

When the townspeople decided to build a bridge to replace the ferry service, which ran over a flat stretch of the river, the unpeopled island became a candidate for development as its fortuitous placement finally dawned on the townspeople. The surveyors' report was ambivalent, however, preferring a longer and less affordable alternative at a site where the river was less deep. Pressed on the matter by the skeptical town selectmen, the surveyor mentioned the "unsteady nature" of the island's geologic structure, and the "inherent difficulties" in building the underlayment for bridge supports or pylons. These vagaries eventually went unchallenged, and the town pursued an alternative. So, the island remained as it was.

After they built the bridge, the river shifted, forming a washboard of rapids in the shallows near town. Boat traffic became dangerous. Near the island, though, the river rose and formed even deeper pools, attractive to boaters who fished for recreation. Boiling currents swelled in an irregular way, however, sometimes with so much force that the river's flow reversed for up to an hour or more, pushing boats away from the rocky shore and back to the dangerous open stretch that ran by town.

One year, the local saloon sponsored a canoe race to mark the start of summer and sell beer, as by ordinance the consumption of whiskey was prohibited out of doors. The brewery erected a large banner on a makeshift pier south of the island, and a crowd gathered there and along the bluffs overlooking the west channel around the island. This was the finishing line of the route for the race, chosen both for the view from the bluffs and the smoother, straighter line the river took through the west channel.

A festival atmosphere descended. They roasted two pigs and a cow and built a stage for antic skits and musicians to perform. There were contests for the making and eating of baked goods. The selectmen saw this as a moment to press civic pride, and speeches opened the event with visions of a town ambitious to grow to such a size on both sides of the river that a train would become not merely desirable but inevitable. Boom times were ahead, and the town looked forward to its place in the mosaic of the nation.

The starting line was roughly a half mile upstream from the island, one hundred yards from shore and just past the rapids. There were two canoeists per team. Once the mayor called them to order and fired the starting shot, they trundled rapidly to the water, portaging the canoes through a roped off chute, with cheering crowds on either side shouting "huzzahs" all around.

The teams slipped skillfully into the water in a tight group. A short distance from shore the main current snatched them up one by one and pulled them into a line. The current combined with the now furious expertise of the canoeists, and they plunged downstream towards the island. The crowd on the bluff began to jump, waving their hats overhead with many a shouted "C'mon, boys!"

Close together as they approached the island, the group aimed for the straighter right channel, but one of the boiling currents surfaced. The line of canoes flattened and split. This contrary current failed as quickly as it arrived, and the canoes surged forward. The bulk of them shot right—some ten or eleven—but three of the canoes were just far enough left of the island's knife-like point that the surge of current back into its usual course pulled them into the narrower curve of the left channel, and they slipped out of view. The crowd at the starting line watched them fade into shadow; those cheering heartily on the bluff saw nothing; and those waiting expectantly at the finish line were completely unaware of these events.

Back at the starting line, the race organizers conferred seriously, wondering whether this would mean disqualification for some, with one proposing a handicapping advantage of sorts to any of the three that could win, place, or show, since they all agreed the left channel was not only longer but more treacherous in an undefined way.

At the finish line, the festival goers, taking cues from the shouts of the crowd on the bluff, hushed and gazed intently at the opening of the intended channel. Time slowed. It seemed that the canoeists should have already appeared. Then in a burst of paddles and effort, the main group of canoes arrived, pulling faster and faster, their boats sunk deep in the rolling center current of the river. One, two, three the winners crossed the line and paddled to shore, with more cheers raised on the bluff and at the pier.

As the crowd greeted the canoes with congratulations, the other three in the far channel emerged. They did not paddle. An eddy spun the canoes like silent tops. Each contestant sat upright and unmoving, trailing their paddles in the water, faces drained and staring. After a shocked pause, canoeists still in the water rallied, paddling across the river to intercept their friends. The organizers launched a rowboat as well, and they caught the errant canoes and towed them back to shore.

These canoeists were silent and soaked to the skin. The race organizers quickly dispensed with regulations, and offered the somnambulant paddlers strong spirits, hot coffee, and blankets. Since the canoeists would not speak, the mayor finally pressed them to explain what had happened.

"It's awful dark on that side of the island," said one, and the others only nodded in agreement.

The new bridge was completed, sited away from the unpeopled island, and had the intended effect. The town grew wildly on both sides of the river, excepting the bluffs overlooking the island and, of course, on the unpeopled island itself. Like the island, the bluffs became wild places, not even park-like, but rustic and overgrown. The few who ventured up them came back discouraged by the brambles and nettles that grew there. Several stands of trees began to thicken in places. The houses and buildings that backed up to the bluffs drew a stark line between the town's habitated gardens, lawns, and well-used commercial space and this wilderness at its heart. From a distance, the bluffs appeared as an extension of the island, spilling inhospitably against the town from the inside.

Since the town had reached such a size, the selectmen decided to commission a decorative map they could publish in hopes of cementing its identity, perhaps as far as New York and Washington. This would include the original Old Town, the primarily residential and vibrant section on the far side of the river (unimaginatively dubbed "the New Town"), and the adjacent cultivated farmland. Parts of both the Old Town and New Town had spread around the base of the bluffs near the island and down the river on either side, and the town completely surrounded the island and its environs. Less distinguished houses and a few warehouses on cheaper land outside the commercial district filled this southerly zone, but it was felt they nonetheless comprised principal elements and would be rendered on the map in equal detail.

This left the island, surrounded now on all sides by the town. How should it be represented on the map?

Some argued for a map illustrated in a medieval style, with the island presented as a stylized refuge, an Edenic garden of animals and trees. The idea of the island, and the bluffs that had become its extension, was just this force and power of the wild land, which the town had subdued into orderly progress and abundance. An illuminated presentation would preserve this idea. And since it was visually quite difficult to imagine the unpeopled island as anything but almost the center of the map (not quite centered) such artistic license would allow the cartographer more aesthetic flexibility. Perhaps the vantage would be from the side, showing the Old Town, the bluffs and island beyond, and then, by playing with perspective, the New Town elevated in the background.

Others demanded strict accuracy with an aerial perspective to capture the town layout, presenting not only the details of its development and extent, but the distinct qualities of each section. Like rings in the stump of a tree, the growth over time could be read in extensions to roads and the additions to Old Town, followed by the bridge, and then New Town's ascension. In this version of the map, however, critics of the aerial perspective saw the island as evidence of failure, an obstacle that had blocked the organic expansion of the town. Supporters claimed it showed the town's power to overcome.

The citizens prominent in business wanted a map that featured a general presentation of the entire town with key sites highlighted and directional arrows locating them. Major commercial sites and the geography of the town's culture—the opera house, the town hall, churches, schools, the river, the bridge—could float above, a tableau of achievement tied by directional arrows to the specificity of the orderly town below.

In the end, the town selectmen forwarded all these suggestions to the cartographer, a man named Elgerson. Elgerson was a meek person who had remained silent through the entire, sometimes acrimonious process. His full-time occupation was county engineer, but he had started as a draftsman, and he was known to possess great patience and excellent attention to detail. A confirmed bachelor, his hobbies included wildlife photography and the occasional watercolor, which he sold to the householders in New Town, where they adorned kitchens and bathrooms.

Everyone expected a muted compromise of sorts, an amalgamation or hybrid that would succeed in most ways and inoffensively disappoint everyone. Rather than hector the poor man, the mayor and selectmen let him be, affording him all the time he needed, which turned out to be twenty-eight days.

The mayor and selectmen sat at a long table, and the townspeople were in rows behind them. Elgerson walked to the front of the room, which suddenly had the strange air of a courtroom. The man had an uncharacteristic authority about him as he walked to stand at the front. There were his three easels with drafts on large boards concealed under sheets.

"Fellow citizens," Elgerson began, then paused and let the crowd silence itself. It took a few moments, and finally the mayor had to turn and cough loudly at someone standing in the doorway.

"I found all the proposals compelling in one regard or another," Elgerson continued, "and since the town afforded me such a luxury of time, and I was relieved of all other duties, well..." and here he broke off and stood awkwardly.

"Perhaps I should just show you what I've done with *your* ideas," Elgerson said, putting an emphasis on "your" that was hard to interpret. He then pulled off the sheets covering the drafts, which fluttered to the floor around the easels.

The first map was clearly the concept proposed by those citizens prominent in business, as there were circled landmarks floating above the town, tethered, so it seemed, by directional arrows. The map rendered the town below in a slight aerial perspective, but in effect it looked like a plate of scrambled eggs or a knitted place-setting, albeit a detailed one with houses and streets. The landmarks, though clearly rendered, seemed inconsistent with the original proposal. Instead of the bridge, town hall, or any other prominent features of cultural significance, Elgerson cataloged elements of street and landscaping. Curbs and gutters, an outhouse, and a small clutch of copper beeches hovered over the town. A selection of mailboxes represented New Town. The unpeopled island in the river was visible solely as a mound of green and brown color.

The second map was the strictly accurate aerial perspective, and it was packed with excruciating detail. So realistic and subtle was the drawing that it raised questions whether Elgerson had suspended himself from a balloon or photographed the town. The accuracy was so great that it captured people out walking, caught mid-stride or turning to wave at someone eating breakfast on their porch. Horses shook their manes, trees bent back under strong breezes. A child held both hands to its face in joyous surprise as a fire engine roared past.

In this version, Elgerson had carefully omitted the unpeopled island and its associated environs. The space remained, but none of the detail, rendering it a lightless void. This revealed that the outline of all that could be called "the unpeopled island and its associated environs" had the shape of a human skull.

The third map was in the illuminated medieval style. The sections of the town ranged in loosely sequential planes of depth, rendered distinct and identifiable. This effect gave the town an immediately comprehensive appearance, sweeping and vibrant, peppered with marginal icons—canoes, beer kegs, farming equipment, antique rifles, a barrel of whiskey—that captured the frontier spirit of the town's earlier days. Elgerson had even woven a filigreed braid of gold and silver that spanned a hand's width at the edge.

The unpeopled island, however, was absent. In its place, centered above the midline of the map, was a black sphere with subtle shading that suggested a reflective material, such as obsidian or onyx. Within the sphere there was an ambiguously gendered figure in white, one hand raised, palm extended.

As if this outrageous nonsense were not enough, there was the figure's expression. One might have called it "blank" or "flat," but it went beyond that, beyond even something like "you can read there what you will" or "enigmatic" or even "indifferent." It was the face of something opaque and alien. But to describe it that way was also a lazy dodge and evasion.

The face, the emblem of what would otherwise have been the unpeopled island in the river, held itself in absolute alterity. It was the face of judgment.

After the debacle with the maps, the mayor and the selectmen hired a balloonist who photographed the town (badly) from a spot just to the south. The balloonist-photographer added labels (the town's name, its most grossly discrete parts) and they were done. Elgerson simply faded back into his life as a county engineer, drawing schematics for new roads and the burgeoning storm water run-off control projects the road paving required.

The map-photograph, however, was a hit. It did, in fact, circulate as far as New York and Washington. An envoy of the town was able to lobby people of influence, who in turn included the town on another map, one for future railway expansion. The mayor quickly had this new railway map, mounted and framed, placed in his office next to the map-photograph. His wife suggested that perhaps the railway map could be adjusted for scale and super-imposed over the map-photograph, but a preliminary effort showed this would just add a set of railroad tracks over the map-photograph. The idea was abandoned, to the relief of everyone except the mayor's wife.

After five years of concept planning, regional planning, legislative funding, surveying, public comment, and feasibility studies, railway construction began. Two years later, the new rail line approached from the horizon, its sections crawling over the plains with a buzzing flurry of encroaching activity. One bright day, it became visible from the town, a hive of cranes, dust, and workers.

The town met the prospect of rail connection to large cities with dreams of travel and tourism, commerce and expansion, culture and opulence. This was their destiny.

In general outline, this prediction seemed accurate. The mayor was quick to point to the western United States, where all the major cities had sprung from the life blood of rail, and to the expansion of European cities, tightly knit on a web of the same stuff. Even China, he noted, could not resist the powerful stimulation of trains. The new railway map had prophesied this greatness.

On the other, smaller map-photograph, though, the new rail line was a problem. Throughout the concept planning, regional planning, legislative funding, surveying, and even the public comment and feasibility studies, the logic of the new railway map held sway, ignoring the reality of the map-photograph. When they finally reconciled the new railway map and the old map-photograph, the town discovered that on the map-photograph the rail line would go straight through Old Town, across the unpeopled island in the river, and on to New Town and beyond.

No one wanted to discuss this fact except for the mayor's wife, and then with a certain rueful tone in her voice.

The day arrived when railway construction crews with flatbed trucks and hulking earth-moving machines combed through the established right of way in Old Town, making a cut through the bluffs down to the river's edge. With perfect timing, barges with gravel and concrete arrived and surrounded the island. The railway crews built a complex series of arches in the Swiss style around the island's rock outcropping, topped by a lattice of steel that formed the railway bridge. Then, they were on to the New Town, where the rail line consumed what little farmland remained near the bluffs.

As quickly as they arrived, the crews were gone.

The mayor announced the opening of the rail line. The greater powers had scheduled a momentous first run. A special train carrying the people of influence who had conceived and executed the construction of the rail line was set to travel its entire length, with stops at each town and city on the route. The town anticipated with enthusiasm this welcome into the modern world of transportation. The town selectmen and the mayor scheduled a civic event at the station, located in the New Town (a nod to the future). There was to be a parade before the train's arrival, with a brass band, and the usual roasting of two pigs and a cow. The local chapter of the conservation corps would host a shooting contest on the bluff. A delegation from the outskirts of Old Town planned a cakewalk, despite the mayor's wife's objection that it was a "vulgar entertainment."

There was hesitant discussion of another canoe race to coincide with the arrival of the train. People again considered the significance of the island, a subject they had so far avoided (with the exception of the mayor's wife). The direction of the train's route meant it would stop in New Town and then proceed over the bridge, that used the island as a central element of support, perched atop a complex filigree of steel beams. The canoeists proposed having the race as the train crossed the river, as a way to make a favorable impression in the minds of the people of influence on board. No one discussed it openly, but they all remembered the earlier canoe race fiasco, and the unsettled opinions the town held respecting the unpeopled island and its associated environs.

During the new railway process, from concept planning to actual construction, no one had dared voice these concerns about the island. Only the mayor's wife had mentioned it in occasional (and rueful) discussion of the new railway map that had started the entire process. Now, however, a dull furor began to build, and previously unthought anxiety formed into speculation. They could do nothing. The completed rail line ran right over the island. Without mentioning anything specific, the mayor reassured everyone. Was there not a process? Had there not been concept planning, regional planning, and many other things conducted by people of influence? Surely, they had constructed the rail line to the highest possible standards, and any unspoken concerns about its relationship to the island were superstitious nonsense or outright simple-minded backwardness that had no place in the town as it ushered in this new stage of development.

Worried but oddly mundane rumors still spread, working into hushed exchanges until they became widely known. What would happen in spring when the river reached flood stage, and the ice sheets piled along the island's rocky shore? Was the rock outcropping stable enough? Would the wildlife on the island, through simple natural action, cause unforeseen damage to the bridge and rail line?

A few of these rumors went further, however, alleging that the "influence" of the island itself was inhospitable to progress. Had it not held itself apart from the town, claiming for itself the otherwise prime real estate on the bluffs? Darker still, one or two people with good memories recalled the debacle of Elgerson's three uncanny maps, apparently produced under this "island influence," most especially the mysteriously threatening angelic figure in the sphere of shining black whose face held an indifference so great as to exceed animosity. The most appalling and absurd of these rumors, which the mayor dismissed as "tittle-tattle," insinuated that Elgerson himself was in "league with" the island and would either attempt to sabotage the bridge in an attack on the people of influence, or, perhaps even more dreadfully, commit suicide off the bridge in plain view of the train as it passed, leaving nothing but shame. Such an event would forever mark the town and its reputation.

This last notion seemed unlikely. Elgerson had entered into semi-retirement from engineering and was now a well-liked portrait painter among the New Town elites, having moved from watercolors to oils. Among the more rural folk who lived in the less desirable parts of Old Town, however, he was regarded as a "queer figure," practically the same as the island itself.

In the end, the town banned all boat traffic on the river the day of the celebratory first run, using the excuse that the shooting contest made it unsafe. Someone suggested that the contestants could shoot at the wildlife on the island as a prophylactic against future damage to the rail line, but organizers forbid this for common sense reasons. As for Elgerson, he had already planned to visit his sister in Chicago to aid in her recovery from elective surgery. Still, these assurances did not relieve anyone of whatever underlying fear about the island had settled on the town. More properly, this fear had always been there, or perhaps it had formed with the town. Fate had woven this dread with its elements, all of which it held in relation to the unpeopled island in the river.

The day of the train's arrival was met with questionable weather, a low sky with cool wind and the threat of rain. Undeterred, the various committees set about their work roasting two pigs and a cow and rolling barrels of beer. The organizers set up the shooting range on the bluffs, and a farmer ran a brush-cutter to prepare a path and areas for the contestants and spectators. The band rehearsed, and someone hired youths to run white ropes between the light poles along the parade route. At the new train station, they constructed a dais at one end of the platform, with a lectern and the photograph-map and the new railway map arranged on easels.

The train was due at 2:30 PM, and by 1:30 PM there was a large, well-fed crowd along the parade route. Organizers declared the winner of the shooting contest. They handed out the cakes from the cakewalk. The town selectmen called for more barrels of beer. The parade began, and the band marched as they played "King Cotton" along the route. As they pulled up to the dais, the band broke into "The Invincible Eagle," one of the mayor's favorites. At exactly 2:27 PM, a child stationed in the Baptist church belfry espied the train and blew his trumpet, a signal that sent the crowd into cheers and huzzahs.

The train's arrival was grand and imposing, and the crowd stilled as the influential passengers disembarked to greet the mayor. They spoke softly to him on the dais, and he offered brief thanks, and shook their hands again. Since there was a schedule to keep, they kept this meeting brief. The mayor and the influential passengers waved to the cheering crowd. Then the passengers quickly returned to the train car. The train departed at exactly 2:35.

More cheers came from the crowd as the train rolled through the cut in the bluff down to the river's edge. All had gone well, and for a moment all fear about the unpeopled island in the river was gone. But then the train crept onto the bridge. The entire town had gathered at the station, and the vantage down the tracks through the cut in the bluffs gave them a clear view of the train, the bridge, and the tracks beyond. The island was not visible beneath the tracks and web of steel.

The train was accelerating on its way, but as it crossed the bridge it slowed, then stopped, as if something mechanical had misfired. The crowd stared blankly. The band had begun to play again (unimaginatively "Merrily We Roll Along") but sputtered unevenly and trailed out as the conductor dropped his hands.

A window on the train opened, then another, then more. The crowd at the station could see hands fumbling to lower them. A head appeared and then several more, turning to talk and gesturing enigmatically. At least one of the heads vomited. The crowd was completely silent.

After a full minute, without closing the windows, the train crept forward, not accelerating but pulling itself one car length at a time. It took another five minutes to disappear.

Reports came the next day that at the subsequent stop all passengers disembarked from the train and traveled over land by car to their point of departure. The empty train continued to the terminus without stopping. When official rail service commenced, the town learned the schedule marked it as a "local" stop on a train which ran only once a day, every three days. While commercial exports from the town were initially significant, the costs were prohibitive and land transport alternatives remained cheaper. Tourist travel to the town by train was minimal, and eventually the local service ran only once a week. Rather than fuel a period of new growth, the train served increasingly as a reminder that the world around the town was more alive, or at least more civilized.

The mayor lost the next election, and his wife filed for divorce. Large corporate agricultural firms purchased the land on all sides, cutting off town expansion. The old families moved away, and the housing stock gradually decayed. The town became a dilapidated clump of housing along the train tracks. The unpeopled island and the bluffs grew wild and thick with turkeys.

Elgerson remained in Chicago. After his sister died, he continued to live in her house, an imposing Second Empire affair with a black slate mansard roof and a large garden. Society types celebrated his still lifes of roses, which he painted from plants that grew in the well-tended beds around the house. He lived to the age of seventy-five. Diagnosed with cancer, and facing the prospect of a lonely death, he shot himself.

The housekeeper found him the next morning, face down in a patch of brambles and nettles that grew in a far corner of the garden.

How I Saved My Marriage

T he worst thing for a marriage is to say it needs saving.
Robert thought that things had been going well enough.
That's what he told his therapist, anyway, and he wasn't wrong. Well enough. You can't expect every day to be perfect, he thought. You can't even expect every day to be above average, right? That's how averages work.

But Robert's wife, Millicent (he always loved her old-fashioned name), she was the reason he was seeing a therapist. Not in the sense that she made him crazy. She just said, "You need to see a therapist," and she wasn't kidding. Not that Robert was crazy, but Millicent wanted him to see a therapist. She had her reasons.

It started in the usual way: Boredom. Millicent had her routine: Feed the cats, empty the dishwasher, clean the cat litter, start the laundry, eat some breakfast, go to work. And one day she noticed. Something was missing from her life. At first, she thought it was just an emotional hangover from the pandemic. She had colleagues and friends who felt the same way, or at least she thought they did. They were bored or unhappy, couldn't find the same energy, hated their jobs. But when Millicent listened to them complain, it seemed they still had something they liked. They were motivated to do *something*.

"We just keep plugging along," a client said after a meeting on zoom. "At least we've been gardening lately. It gets us out of the house. Maybe one day I'll feel normal again."

"I've got to get home," her assistant said after dropping off some papers. "We're going to my parents, and Jim wants to clean the car first. I started drinking Starbuck's Frappuccinos during the pandemic. I love them, but I keep leaving the cans in the front seat. It drives him nuts. I have no idea why I do it."

Millicent stared at her reflection. Maybe gardening or Frappuccinos would do it. She studied the lines of her face, the spatter of small freckles on her forehead.

Things aren't the same, she thought, but *I'm* still the same.

She pulled gently at the corner of her eye. The crow's feet definitely starting to show, but *just* starting. Just barely.

And then, behind her, through the open door, she watched Robert walk by. He was wearing his "cat pants," short-legged pajamas from Japan he'd bought off some website. Shirtless, he held his phone up to his face, reading glasses in one hand.

And then it struck her. It was Robert. He was different.

She started a mental review, noticing exactly how different. The Peloton bicycle gathering dust. Infrequent shaving. When was the last time they went out to dinner? And how many times had he fed the cats? Or emptied the dishwasher? Changed the cat litter?

When they ate dinner, he sat quietly, just eating. Did he ever ask about her day? Did he ever say anything? And what about sex? He had a habit of watching her shower, but it never led to anything. Not that it mattered anymore.

"You need to see a therapist," she told him that night at dinner. "I made you an appointment."

"Like, go see a therapist?" Robert said. "At their office?"

"Yes."

"Don't they have that online?" he said.

"I got a referral from a friend," Millicent said. "This therapist works with people like you."

Robert considered asking what "people like you" meant but decided not to.

Robert, for his part, was as clueless as this all sounds. He really was. And it wasn't inertia or the pandemic or getting a "bit stale." It was active decay.

"You really need to see a therapist," Millicent said.

And that was that.

Surprisingly, it went well. The therapist, a tall, thin man named Alan, emphasized "letting it out," and "not filtering anything."

"This is a confidential space for you," he said. "I'm not going to judge. I'm not going to shut you down. Just whatever you're holding on to, let it go."

It took a few sessions, but Robert enjoyed it. He didn't have a lot of friends, and Alan seemed interested in just about anything he had to say. Robert even looked forward to Thursday afternoons. There was a Taco Bell on the way, so he would grab a 3 crunchy Tacos combo (with a Diet Coke) and eat it in the parking lot listening to a podcast on anime, then talk with Alan for an hour about whatever he was thinking. Afterwards he might go look at comic books or head over to Best Buy and dream about a nicer TV. The whole thing tired him out, so he would take a nap before dinner.

Millicent didn't notice any change, except that Robert indeed looked forward to the sessions, planned for them, even mentioned them beforehand. This, it seemed, was progress.

"So, it's good?" she asked, hopefully.

"Yeah," he said. "Yeah, I think it's helping."

Six weeks after starting therapy, Robert woke up in the middle of the night. It was raining, and there was a thunder-less flash of lightning that lit up the bedroom with stark incandescence. The image floated in his eyes for a moment, and as it faded he saw something moving just outside the bedroom door, gliding away. Millicent? No, she was asleep, sprawled on her side with the covers kicked down at her feet, one arm dangling off the bed.

Robert got out of bed, tiptoeing to the door. He stood there, with one hand on the wall, listening. Nothing. Stepping into the hall, he peered over the railing and down into the living room. There, over by the bay window, he saw it again, something white and floating like a curtain. But they didn't have curtains. They had those "Roman shades"

Millicent had gone on about for months, and they were pulled all the way up.

He froze. If he went downstairs, whoever or whatever it was would see him coming. They would have the jump on him.

"Who's there?" he whispered theatrically from the top of the stairs, crouching down to get a better look. Just the fluttering white floating by the window. But he could see something below. Were those feet? Bare feet? He stood up and began to descend the stairs. Halfway down, another flash of lightning filled the room with light. In that instant, he saw the form of a woman, hovering by the window, her outline visible through the loose gown she was wearing.

"Who are you?" Robert whispered, continuing down the stairs.

The figure floated with her arms out, head lolling to one side. The light from the porch caught the side of her face, and Robert could see the slightest smile. Her eyes glistened under heavy lids, moving side to side as if following some unseen object. As Robert stared at her, an inexplicable warmth flooded him, something like joy.

Then, she was gone.

Robert stood for a minute, stunned, his breath coming fast, pulse hammering in his ears. He sat down on the sofa, then lay down and folded his arms over his chest, as the shock refused to wear off. Suddenly, he stood up and went to the bathroom, staring at his face in the mirror. Had his hair gone white? Was there some kind of proof written in his eyes? Nothing. He was the same. He splashed water on his face, drank some from his hands, and sat down on the closed toilet lid. Putting his head between his knees, he began to hyperventilate.

Going back to the mirror, he looked at his face again. Nothing had changed; he was the same as he ever was. Why did he feel so different? He replayed the image of the floating woman in his mind, recalling the detail of her outline, that face, those eyes. It couldn't have been real, but everything about it remained in lurid and unspeakable detail. Now, in memory, he imagined the sound of her shifting gown, the texture of her short-cropped hair, the glistening teeth behind her parted lips.

It was Terri Schiavo. Terri Schiavo had appeared to him. In his living room.

It was 5:45 AM by the time Robert had calmed down. He made some coffee and found a coffee cake in the freezer and popped it in the oven. Then, he went upstairs, showered and shaved, then put on some jeans and a white shirt. Millicent found him in the kitchen.

"I made some coffee cake," he said. "Well, I defrosted it anyway. Coffee?" He poured a cup and held it out to her.

Millicent took the cup and sipped.

"Are you okay?" she said.

"I'm fine, fine," Robert said. "Why?"

"Nothing," Millicent said, shrugging. "You're up early is all."

"Do we need anything at the store?" Robert said. He needed to get out of the house, to think.

"Don't you have therapy today?" Millicent said.

She was right. What would he tell Alan about Terri Schiavo? The need to get out of the house was urgent.

"Yeah," Robert said, trying to be casual. "I was going to go grocery shopping afterwards."

"That's kind of you," Millicent said, pointing to the notepad on the refrigerator. "There's the list. And I guess now we need another coffee cake."

Since it was early, Robert drove aimlessly for about an hour, then went to the Highland Shopping Mall, one of the high-end types with all the stores on either side of a dainty road with slant parking and manicured planters filled with decorative cabbages. He parked and window shopped absentmindedly. It was almost noon, so he ducked into a sushi bar he liked and ate an early lunch perched on a stool in front of the chef. Looking into the gleaming metal and glass cooler at a mackerel lying blank-eyed on a bed of ice, he startled at the reflection of a figure in white standing behind him. It was only the server handing menus to a table. The sushi chef, who Robert knew from previous meals, laughed.

"Careful," the chef said, waving his knife. "You jump around, I'm going to cut my fingers off."

Finally, it was time for therapy. It was a challenge. Alan gave the usual preamble: Let it out, say whatever, confidential space. But a hallucination? Of Terri Schiavo? And afterwards, the shock of it, the strange pleasure of it.

"Something has me shook up," Robert said.

"I noticed you have a lot of pent-up energy," Alan said. Robert fidgeted, crossed his legs.

"I just feel that something's changed," Robert said. "Shifted, you know."

"That's fairly general," Alan said. "Don't filter. Just notice what you're feeling, in your body, right now."

"Well, I woke up in the middle of the night," Robert said. "There was this weird lightning. Very bright, like it was right on top of us, but no thunder."

"Hmm," Alan said. "That is weird."

"Yeah, and afterward I was a bit freaked out," Robert said, "but I felt good. Like, I had a lot of energy. I had to do something, with my hands."

"Motivated?"

"Yeah, that's it. I felt motivated. So, I made coffee, some coffee cake, showered, everything," Robert said in a rush. "I 'started my day,' so to speak. It was only 6:00 AM. I haven't felt like that in a long time."

"A couple things," Alan said. "Just putting this out there, okay? We've talked a lot about doing things as a way of helping change your mood. Noticing how you feel when you do things and noticing when you feel distress."

"I wasn't distressed," Robert said. "I just felt *better* somehow."

The parking lot at Ralph's was almost empty and Robert parked near the front door. He grabbed a cart and headed for the produce section. The cart's front right wheel wobbled and kept sticking, but he marched on, the cart veering occasionally. Celery, carrots, onions. Maybe he'd make soup. Parsley, potatoes. Have to get some beans and some chicken stock.

Robert was staring at the bananas when, out of the corner of his eye, he noticed something white on the floor disappear around a corner into the Ethnic Foods aisle. He'd managed to get Terri Schiavo out of his mind during therapy, but here she was, creeping back in. But it couldn't happen here, in the grocery store. There would be witnesses. What if he was just crazy? If he was psychotic, it could happen anywhere. Robert imagined himself in a YouTube video, "Crazy Man Thinks Terri Schiavo is in Grocery Store." He had been able to act normally in front of Millicent, and at therapy. Maybe that would work here, too. He could just ignore it. But that feeling, the effect she had had on him that morning was so strong, overpowering. He still had no words that captured the intensity and warmth. It was strange, but it felt *good*, spiritual and also, in a way, almost physical.

He could take a look down the aisle, and if she was there, he could just skip it. He didn't need anything from Ethnic Foods, anyway.

Robert pushed the cart around the corner, and the aisle was empty. He remembered what Alan had said. How did he feel now, staring at an empty aisle of Mexican boxed dinners and salsa? Disappointed. He felt disappointed that there was no ghostly Terri Schiavo floating in the Ethnic Foods aisle at Ralph's.

Robert put the groceries away and went to his home office to work. He made technical drawings for a CNC manufacturer of custom assembly-line parts and had almost finished a set of injection valves for a shampoo bottling machine. They were due at the end of the week. The large desk where he worked had his desktop and the robot pen plotter he used for his drawings. The only decoration in the room was a framed poster for the anime "Promise of Another Day," with the main character, Miki, smiling brightly at a butterfly resting on a flower's petals. It was his favorite, but now, looking at Miki's eyes, her moistened teeth, the flowing gown and outstretched arms, it unsettled him. Taking the frame down, he turned it towards the wall and got to work.

"You're still working?" Millicent said, standing in the doorway.

"Yes," Robert said,

"It's 7:30," she said. "Did you eat lunch?"

"Yes," Robert said. "Before therapy."

"And you came back here and just worked?"

"No, I stopped at Ralph's," he said. "I bought some steak for dinner. Sorry I didn't get it started. I must have lost track of time. Almost finished with these."

"I thought they weren't due until Friday?"

"I was on a roll," Robert said. "I'll call and get some more projects."

Millicent went back to the living room to make some phone calls, then she reviewed a spreadsheet covering construction costs on a project. She heard Robert banging around in the kitchen.

"Now what are you doing?" she said, opening the refrigerator.

"Starting dinner," Robert said, smiling. "Nothing fancy, just some pasta sauce. We'll have steak tomorrow. Would you like a glass of wine?"

"No, I'm good for now," Millicent said. "What's gotten into you?"

Robert straightened up.

"Nothing," he said. "Just making pasta sauce."

After dinner that night, they sat down to watch television. Robert put his arm around Millicent along the back of the sofa.

"What do you want to watch?" he said.

"Downton Abbey," she said. "I know you hate it but—"

"Okay," Robert said, switching the channel.

Millicent mimed shock.

"What?" Robert said. "I don't think I gave it a chance."

That night, Robert curled up next to Millicent and she fell asleep while he stroked her hair.

After breakfast the next day, Robert decided to get the car washed. It was a 2016 Subaru Crosstrek with ice silver metallic paint, which unfortunately showed road grime more than he liked. Millicent used it most since she had meetings with clients and down at city hall, and Robert only ran a few errands, like mailing drawings. He still liked it to be clean, even getting the "new car" scent despite Millicent objecting.

Robert pulled the car into the line for interior cleaning and rolled down the window.

"Welcome to Gung Ho Car Wash," said a smiling, pot-bellied man in blue coveralls, holding out a laminated sheet. "Our mission is to serve you. Would you like the supreme, deluxe, or everyday package? We're having a special on the deluxe, with undercarriage spray and hot wax included."

"Um," Robert said, considering. "Let's go with the deluxe."

"Excellent choice. Scent?" the man said. "Black Frost, Fruit Medley, Pine Forest, New Car?"

Robert thought for a moment.

"You know what," he said, "let's skip the scent this time."

"Please turn on your hazards," the man said, scrawling on the windshield with a chunk of white wax and handing Robert a ticket.

At the entrance to the car wash, another man sprayed the car's sides with foam and pointed to the instructions hanging from the ceiling, "Engine on, Car in neutral," then sprayed the windshield. With a slight jerk, the roller grabbed the car and began to pull it through. Blue and white rollers came from both sides, and a red one dropped to the hood, all of them sliding along together with a pleasant rumbling sound. An array of nozzles sprayed next, rinsing the foam. The sound and familiar smells were a comfort. The undercarriage wash was next, a special section framed in by a metal box. A light display switched on, flashing "UNDERCARRIAGE" as the car rolled by.

And then Robert saw her. Terri Schiavo was standing—floating?—at the next station, the hot wax. It was another special section, with a frame of sheet metal boxes on either side and red neon lights. Terri was next to the wall in front of the lights. As they turned on, they revealed the outline of her body, as the lightning had done, but now somehow dire and more exquisitely detailed in the vivid glow. Again, her head lolled slightly from side to side, and Robert felt her gaze vaguely shift from the hood over the roof. As he passed by in the unhurried pace of the car wash roller, he stared at her face and shuddered at both the mystery and mundane reality of his vision. How could this be happening?

The car proceeded to the blowers, beads of water rolling up the windshield, along the windows, until it came to an end. The red light turned green, and one of the workers waved Robert to an exit bay and signaled for him to stop. Robert stepped out, and the worker took the ticket from him and pointed to the waiting room. Inside, Robert paid and then sat nervously eating free popcorn. When the man cleaning the interior of the car stood up and waved a rag to signal it was finished, Robert stood hurriedly and stuffed a five-dollar bill in the tip box, then shuffled out to the car, nervously glancing back at the car wash line. Steam billowed like ocean waves, and suds tumbled in the drainage sluice.

One time at the car wash, the pot-bellied man had told him that almost all the water the car wash used was recycled and reused.

While he was waiting for some new projects, Robert got on the Peloton. Checking the workout history, he saw it had been over six months since his last class. Six months. What the hell, Robert thought. He chose a half hour power zone class, and halfway through almost quit, but then the music changed to classic rock, so he powered through the climbs.

At one point, he thought he saw something around the corner, something white and faintly diaphanous, but he ignored it. He was in his groove, and on the leader board.

The next day, after another Peloton class, shower and shave, and taking out the garbage, Robert sat down with a new set of drawing specs, this time a tricky project for the automated manufacture of flippers on a donut machine. He sank right into it. Around 2:00 PM he realized he'd skipped lunch and decided to make a tuna salad sandwich. He couldn't remember the last time he'd had one, and his mouth actually watered at the prospect. There was that sourdough bread from Ralph's, the kind with sesame seeds, and a can of Cento tuna in olive oil that would be perfection.

As he opened the can, however, a single drop of oil spattered up on his tie—Robert had decided to wear a tie today, no reason—and he groaned. He rinsed and dried his hands then slipped the tie off and blotted it with a paper towel, wondering if they had any corn starch to pre-treat the stain. Distracted for a moment, he was shocked when he looked up and Terri Schiavo was there, right in front of him, in broad daylight. Thankfully, Millicent had an on-site meeting.

Robert put the tie on the counter and backed away, stumbling at the door sill. Terri Schiavo floated by the door to the basement, motionless except for the slight nodding of her head side to side. Then, slowly but deliberately, her left hand rose, one finger extended pointing to the door. The door, held open by a brick in the gap, swung out all the way. After a tense moment, Terri Schiavo floated through the door and disappeared. Unsure what to do, Robert followed.

At the head of the stairs, he switched on the light and went down. The basement was unfinished, filled with boxes along the walls and the mechanicals nestled in one corner. The single bulb threw a cone of light in the center, but all else was shadows, and he couldn't see Terri Schiavo anywhere. Something shifted, like a sheet of cardboard sliding on concrete, right under the stairs. He peered through the open risers and there she was, her hand pointing again, this time at the cat litter box. In a rush of excitement, Robert bounded down the last few steps and stumbled into a plastic container filled with Christmas ornaments. Regaining his balance, he turned to look, but she was gone.

Robert ate his sandwich with shaking hands. What did it mean? In so many ways, this was worse than before, worse even than the spectacular vision in the car wash. She was *there*, in his kitchen. It was immediate, concrete. It was real. It had to mean something. But what? What did any of it mean? More than that, how did it make him feel? That's what Alan had said, to notice how distress made him feel in his body. But it wasn't distress. It was energy. It made Robert want to act, do something important. It made him feel strong.

Robert ate the rest of his sandwich purposefully, put his dishes in the dishwasher, and went to the basement. He lifted the lid of the cat box and began to scoop. After a moment, he realized that this wouldn't do: He needed to clean the entire thing. Grabbing a plastic bag, he carefully emptied the box, then carried both to the garage. He double bagged the used litter—you can't be too careful—and then went to the driveway and hosed out the box.

Later, Millicent poked her head into Robert's office.

"Whoa," she said. "What's the occasion? You got your fancy duds on today."

"Nothing," Robert said, looking up. "Just, you know, what Keats said."

"No, I don't know what Keats said."

"Put on a clean shirt, tie your shoes," Robert said. "That kind of thing. It helps you work. How was your meeting?"

"Okay, usual nonsense," Millicent shrugged, and disappeared. A minute later, she poked back in.

"Did you clean the cat litter?" she said. Robert nodded without looking up.

"I mean, did you clean the whole thing," Millicent continued. Robert nodded again. Millicent made a puzzled face and then went away.

It was time for a haircut, Robert thought. Usually, he went to the barbershop next to a furniture store on Route 41. It was only ten bucks, and they had a stack of Playboys he liked to leaf through, old ones with folds and tears and advertisements for cigarettes and CB radios. Once he'd gone to Sport Cuts, but the whole vibe was off, and the woman gave him a scalp massage he found disquieting. There was a salon called Maison he had noticed driving to Ralph's the other day, an upscale interior decorator in a building with tasteful windows above. He paused before going upstairs, admiring the new kitchen on display in the window.

His hairdresser, Karen, was an affable but low-key person, who talked evenly about her family vacation and asked the right questions. She explained how his hair grew, the types of cuts that would work best, even complimented the small patch of gray in his "forelock."

"We could keep it longer on top," she said. "Highlight the gray."

"Highlight it?" Robert said.

"Sure," Karen said. "I mean, people pay for that. You're lucky. It might take a few months to grow in, but it'd be a natural look for you. A side part, fade at the back. Easy."

Robert looked down at the piles of hair in his lap. There were some flecks of gray here and there, not too much. Maybe this "salt and pepper" thing Karen was talking about was good.

When he looked up, Terri Schiavo stared back from the mirror. She was behind Karen, who was trimming his neck, oblivious.

"Hold still," Karen said. "Try not to move."

Terri Schiavo raised both arms, the sides of her white gown billowing, and Robert could swear she smiled. It was the gentlest hint, perhaps a trick of the light or his mind, but he could feel it was a smile. Then he felt something else, a light warmth in his chest. Karen was talking, but Robert felt he could hear someone else, the sound of another voice. Not words, not even a tone, but a pattern of meaning. He could hear thoughts. Terri Schiavo's thoughts, explaining everything. This haircut, the clothes, the Peloton, the car wash. Millicent. Everything. It was so clear now, so beautiful and easy. Doused with a solemn joy, Robert closed his eyes in reverie.

"Something is different with Robert," Millicent said.

"Still wearing pajamas all day?" Allison said, stirring her coffee.

"No," Millicent said. "That's what I mean. He's woken up every day at 6:00 for a month, worked out, shaved, put on a tie, and worked through lunch. He's a machine. We even, you know, 'do it' a couple times a week."

"Sweetheart, you don't call that 'different,'" Allison said. "You call that good. 'Different' is a nice way of saying 'weird and goofy.'"

"Remember how he was into anime?" Allison said. "Nope. True crime. He listens to true crime podcasts when he's working out. But he always has his headphones in. 'I don't want to disturb you.' Asks about my day, what I've been doing, when I'll be home. It's different. He was never that way."

"He was a slob."

"No, I mean before Covid," Millicent said. "He wasn't a slob, he just wasn't, I don't know. Mr. Perfect."

"So?"

"So what?"

"What happened?"

"I feel much better," Robert said. "I don't know when I've felt this good."

"That sounds great," Alan said. "You've done a lot of work. It's hard."

"You know," Robert said, "at first, I felt like it was about getting motivated. But it's not. It's about doing things. You just have to do things, and the motivation finds you. I finished nine projects last week. That's twice what I usually get through. I'm up for a promotion."

Alan nodded and took notes.

"How's Millicent?" he asked.

"Seems fine," Robert said, shrugging. "We went out to dinner last week, a little splurge. I ordered champagne and she called me crazy."

"Well, we talked about your anxiety with money," Alan said. "What's changed?"

"I was so busy worrying about money that I wasn't doing anything. I wasn't living."

"So, what do you worry about now?"

Robert thought for a minute.

"Nothing," he said. "I don't have anything to worry about. Not really."

Millicent was upstairs, changing into some sweatpants and a T-shirt. Downstairs, Robert was making dinner, meatloaf from the smell of it. Perfect for Friday night, Netflix, and chill. She thought about it, decided 'no bra,' slipped on the T-shirt, and left the bedroom. At the top of the stairs, she started down quickly, so quickly that she never saw the string tied across the edge of the top step, just a few inches above the carpet. It caught her leg, and she stumbled, lost her balance, then fell forward, tumbling down the stairs. Her head hit the flagstone flooring at the bottom, in front of the door.

In the ICU that night, a grimly cautious doctor entered the small waiting room where Robert sat alone, with a blank expression on his face.

"Mr. Green," the doctor said, pulling up a chair.

"Is it bad?" Robert said.

"Millicent suffered a severe diffuse axonal injury," the doctor said. "That's a kind of brain trauma caused by movement of the brain. There was also bleeding, but we have reduced the pressure. She's in a coma now."

"Is she ever going to wake up?" Robert said, his eyes welling with tears.

"We can't predict that now," the doctor said. "It was—it was a severe injury. We have imaging, but it's still too early to score the severity. You can take all the time you need here and we'll talk later." The doctor rose to leave.

"Can I see her now?" Robert said, wiping his eyes on his sleeve. The doctor thought for a moment, then nodded.

They walked along the dim corridor. Robert could see through a window at the far end of the hall, the first light of dawn rising. The doctor pulled aside a curtain. Millicent lay on the bed, her head bandaged and a ventilator protruding from her mouth. Both eyes were closed and bruised. Machines pumped and beeped in a strangely off-rhythm chorus. A nurse, adjusting some equipment to the left, noticed the doctor and Robert, then backed away from the monitor.

Robert sat in a small chair next to the bed. Millicent's arm dangled slightly off the side. He took her hand and began to cry the most confusing tears.

A Little Gem of a Story

Someone once told me a story, the kind of wild shaggy dog yarn that wanders all over the place promising one thing only to turn you on your head, and itself, too, and probably the person who told it. It was a good story, and I'm trying to remember the details. Bear with me just a minute.

It was actually a ghost story and a pretty good one. I'll remember it all in a second.

No one wants to be able to guess the end of a story, although a lot of people get mad when a story doesn't turn out like they expect it to. Let's be honest: If Godzilla doesn't stomp Tokyo, or if Tarzan doesn't meet Jane, that would disappoint a lot of people. Strangely, people will also complain that a story is predictable. Tough business being a storyteller. People want that something extra, but not extra in a difficult way.

"Well, a story has to be logical," a critic retorts. "It has to have an 'arc of development.'"

Godzilla coming out of a kelp bed and, say, learning to play the piano is just as 'logical' as Godzilla somehow sensing that humans are once again toying with forbidden knowledge. As for development, a montage that shows some kindly spinster lovingly gazing as her giant lizard pupil progresses from "Chop Sticks" to Schumann's "Wild Ride" Op. 68 No. 8 would be fantastic. I would definitely watch that movie and be happy afterwards.

It's easy to spot a regular kind of story.

"I had a three way with some flight attendants," your unpleasant friend confides in a low voice intended to add hilarity to the merely vulgar. Talk about predictable. Sure, lots of "action" (some stories bring you down to their level), but we all know how it ends.

"It's all about the journey," the critic chimes in. "What the characters learn along the way."

125

I mean, okay. Let's go grocery shopping and see what discoveries await. Clean up on aisle 9. Open the carton of eggs: One's broken! You could have some kind of "Moby Dick" interlude that details how expiration dates are calculated for milk. In the end, grandma slowly explains her diagnosis while you stand in the check-out line, methodically thumbing through coupons.

"It's how you tell the story," the critic says, softening their voice for emphasis, a ploy to disguise inanity with misdirection.

You ever read about "the greatest first lines"? Or "the best endings of short stories"? Or the greatest "twist"? Shocking setups, flashbacks, evocative figural language, inventive reworking of narrative, reclaiming voice, fashionable allusions, on and on and on. The critical mind finds no end, no limit to extension, no filter fine enough to gather the effusions proffered for a fiction it finds satisfying. Even worse, the uncritical mind yanks up "I like what I like. Don't read so much into it." Well, at least that's honest, if useless. Go back and reread "Chapter 31 — Queen Mab" from "Moby Dick." Critical and uncritical minds alike are flummoxed. But give those same minds their favorite ice cream and all is well. No accounting for taste.

Here's an idea: Rewrite "Moby Dick" but instead of a whale, Godzilla. Instead of a peg leg, Ahab's is just a lump of roasted flesh. I would read that book. You've already sold one copy.

I've remembered that story, the "on your head one" I mentioned at first that wasn't a shaggy dog story after all but a ghost story. The guy who told it to me, Mack Williams, is a bit of a crank, so he started it out like this one with some kind of nonsense. But when he got down to it, the story didn't wander all that much, although it did turn me on my head.

We were sitting in two wing back armchairs in front of a fire, sipping whiskey.

"People always want to hear a good story," Mack said.

"Well, yes," I said. "You're usually good for one."

Mack is a big man, square headed, with the sharp look of a boxer, although I don't think he ever boxed. His eyebrows droop quite a bit, and he's got a long scar on the back of his head you can see through his close-cropped hair. As a child he was educated in England, but you don't notice until he starts telling a genuinely interesting story, and then it's only because he'll lace some odd expression into it, like "I suspected Tristan was up to something devilish," or "Fiona spent all her money on Balenciaga."

"Do you want to hear it?" Mack said. "The story?"

One of Mack's finer qualities: He doesn't like to bore people, or at least he doesn't like to bore people unwillingly.

"Is it scary?" I asked. "Something that starts 'Have you ever seen a *real* ghost?'"

"It is," Mack said. "That question fits the bill exactly. All stories are really questions, aren't they..." etc. I'll omit the cranky introduction. Here's the remainder, just as Mack told it:

So, there we were, standing by a fresh grave in a light November rain, and Reginald was terrified, I tell you, absolutely jumping out of his skin.

"It's broad daylight," I said. "Get a grip on yourself."

Reginald is tall and thin, with dark hair and pale skin, and it was one of those light rains when the sun cuts through occasionally. You could see the blue veins on the side of his head. He looked absolutely spectral.

"I came around that tree," Reginald said, pointing with a skeletal hand, "and she was lying here, on the grave, crying. She was pawing the earth, all wet and muddy."

"What did you do?" I asked.

"What could I do?" he said. "I watched for about a minute, but she didn't notice me, just kept weeping and rolling around. I jogged off as quietly as I could."

"Why are you telling me all this?" I said. He'd been nervous all during lunch, and then confided he had something to show me, and here we were. Suddenly he turned away and started off to the edge of the cemetery near the road. I walked after him.

"Right there," he said and pointed again, "at that intersection about nine months ago, a foreign graduate student walking home late at night was killed. It was snowing, and two cars had some kind of accident—both of them were sliding around, and one bumped the other right up on the sidewalk. No one was really hurt, and it wasn't at all clear who was at fault. Anyway, in the dark and confusion, none of them noticed that the car had knocked the woman off the sidewalk into that ditch. The drivers settled things quickly and drove off, but she was lying there just out of sight, dying. Perhaps she was already dead."

"That's awful," I said, turning towards the new grave. "But that grave is fresh. And that's a man's name. 'Lysander Kuzma' is a man's name."

"That makes it all the stranger," Reginald said, stopping to stare at me. "Why is a woman's ghost at someone else's grave?"

"We don't *know* it was a ghost," I pointed out. "It was daytime. And look at that part of the cemetery. It's mostly children."

We scanned the section of the cemetery around the fresh grave. Teddy bears and other stuffed animals lay grimly against the gravestones, and here or there faded mylar balloons dangled limply from tree limbs.

"Why can't ghosts come out in the day?" he said. "And why do the children matter?"

"Well, I won't claim to know more about ghosts than most people," I responded, "but generally they seem nocturnal. As for the children, I'd guess those are unplanned burials. Those plots are the cheap seats in this cemetery, so they probably get skipped when people plan ahead. Children's accidents and sudden deaths, or tragic diseases. Junior finds dad's handgun, that sort of thing. The grief must be terrible. A young mother who has lost a child would be out of her head with it."

"Lysander Kuzma," Reginald said, repeating the name on the gravestone. "I looked it up. A suicide. He was twenty-four. A foreign graduate student. Killed himself last week. He was studying physics."

It seemed to me there was a high mortality rate among foreign graduate students that bore investigating, at the very least.

"And I suppose you know who the young woman in the ditch was?"

"Maria Zaytseva," Reginald whispered. "She was studying music and danced ballet."

I didn't want to jump to conclusions; the patchwork of ethnicity meant two Slavic sounding names could be completely unconnected, even historically opposed. It's sort of like calling a place an "Indian burial ground," without getting a specific tribe or nation attached to it. A real tell. But it was curious.

"So let me get this straight," I said as we walked back to the car. "You think this Maria Zaytseva wants you to do something for Lysander Kuzma. Is that right?"

"Yes," Reginald said softly.

"But you don't know what."

"Yes."

"And you want me to help you figure this all out."

"Would you?" he said, sounding hopeful. "I could really use some help."

"Are you sure you just don't feel guilty for jogging away?" I said. "Or maybe you're just sad because a woman was crying on a fresh grave in the rain? That is heart rending."

"No," Reginald said. "Or yes. Wait. What are you asking? I don't feel guilty. And she *was* a ghost. You should have seen her, Mack. The look on her face...."

"All right, then," I told him, concerned by the look on his face. "Let's get on with it."

As you know, I work with a lot of engineers. I'm not an engineer, but you have to admire how they think. Glass half empty or half full? No, just 100% redundant. I called one of my friends, a professor of engineering named Tim, and he'd heard about Kuzma.

"Terrible," Tim said. "He was in Nuclear Engineering. Got his master's last year, just started his PhD. I didn't know him, but he was working for Sujeet, so he must've been good. Good at physics, anyway."

"What's that mean?" I asked.

"Well," Tim said. "Sujeet's good about the work life balance, tries to watch out for the grad students. I don't know if you heard, but we had another suicide a few years ago. Different lab, different professor, but I worry about the culture sometimes. Some of these kids either work too hard or are made to work too hard. You want me to ask Sujeet about it?"

I did, and Tim promised to call me back.

Meanwhile, Reginald had been busy and tracked down the name of Kuzma's housemate.

"He won't call me back," Reginald said. "I keep leaving messages, but nothing. Maybe I should go to his house?"

"Hold on," I told him. "We don't want to scare him off, or worse yet piss him off. His friend just died, Thanksgiving holiday is only a week away. Is he in engineering, too?"

"No," Reginald said. "Slavic Languages and Literatures. Name's Bernard Bochenek. You don't think this is something, I don't know, cultural?"

"For God's sake," I said, "don't be foolish. Maria, Lysander, Bernard. They could all be from different countries. Might not even speak the same languages. Hold on and we'll wait to hear from Tim."

It took until December for Tim to call me. Sujeet had been shocked by Kuzma's death, said he was a "quiet kid who worked hard," a Ukrainian with an aunt in Baltimore.

"Not much else to tell you," Tim said.

And so we had to go see Bochenek, after all.

I briefed Reginald to let me do the talking and more importantly not to mention any ghosts, Maria or otherwise.

It was December 6, around 6:00 in the evening. The weather had turned cold early, and there was a light dust of snow falling. The house was just off Breese Terrace near the stadium, and that hulking thing loomed over us as we shuffled down the sidewalk.

It was a small house, one of dozens of worn-out housing stock students live in, but close to Engineering and probably a lot of fun on game day. It had a sagging porch, loose plastic siding, and a small second story with one dormer on the right side that made the whole affair look off kilter. On the whole, it had a sad face, but it didn't feel haunted. Not at first, anyway.

A small, young balding man with a round face and little square glasses answered the door, blinking under the porch light.

"Can I help you?" he asked in a soft voice.

"I'm Mack Williams," I said, "and this my friend Reginald. We're not police or anything, just interested in Lysander Kuzma and you, actually. My condolences. It must be hard."

"You know who I am?" he said, cautiously, perhaps even fearfully.

"Well, Reggie and I were walking in the cemetery," I said. "We saw Lysander's grave, and when we learned his story Reggie thought, well, we both know how hard it is to be in graduate school, and being a foreign student must be even harder. We thought we'd look in on you, see if there was anything we could do to help. We're both graduates of the university."

This wasn't exactly lying, and to be honest, looking at that young man there, in the half-light of the porch, the swirling snow, the little glasses, it affected me. I felt sorry for him.

He paused for a moment then opened the door with a gesture to enter.

"Come in, please," he said. "Make yourselves at home."

The front room was small, but meticulously neat, with a respectable sofa and two chairs around a second-hand coffee table.

"My name is Bernard Bochenek," he said. "Please, be seated. Would you like some tea? I do not have coffee."

"Yes, please," Reginald said, unfortunately. Bernard nodded once, then silently retreated to the kitchen. He returned almost immediately with a thermos and poured three cups, each with a slice of lemon. "This is how we like it back home. In Poland."

I shot Reginald a glance at that, but he was looking at Bernard intently, almost staring. I coughed softly, and Reginald snapped out of it. We all sat down, Bernard and Reginald on the sofa, while I sat opposite on a chair.

"When did you visit the cemetery?" Bernard asked.

"Weeks ago," I said.

"And you've been calling me," Bernard said, turning to Reginald.

"Uh, well, yes," Reginald said. "Yes, I have."

"I didn't mean anything by it," Bernard said. "Not answering. I have a lot on my mind. I have to find a new place to live."

"Must be tough, paying the entire rent," I said. "We can help with that."

"It's not the rent," he replied.

"Memories?" Reginald offered. Bernard gave him a blank look.

"It's the room," Bernard said. "I haven't gone in since that night. I won't go in it. I don't stay upstairs at night."

The house was small, with the kitchen and the front room taking up the entire ground floor, except for a small toilet just visible before the kitchen.

"So, what then?" Reginald said. "You sleep on the couch?"

"It's a nice couch," Bernard said. "Very comfortable. But I can't live here. I'm leaving in January."

Bernard's attitude changed. He was clearly quite intelligent, observant, and I sensed him sizing us up, especially Reginald.

"What exactly did you see at the cemetery, Mr.—," Bernard said, nodding towards Reginald.

"Jones," Reginald offered.

"What exactly did you see at the cemetery, Mr. Jones?"

So, he had us, just like that. I could tell from the way his eyes sharpened behind those little metal frames that he knew something far more important than we did.

"Go on, then," I said to Reginald.

"Well, I was jogging through the cemetery, first week of November—"

"After Lysander died," Bernard interjected.

"I suppose," Reginald said. "I saw his grave, still fresh. It was raining slightly."

Bernard waited, tenting his hands on his lap.

"Go on," he said.

Reginald looked at me for help, but here we were, and there was nothing else for it.

"And there was a woman, lying on the grave, crying."

At this Bernard drew back, and his color faded slightly. We sat in silence for almost thirty seconds.

"They fought," Bernard said quietly. "Maria and Lysander. I don't know about what. I speak Ukrainian, but Maria was Icelandic. Her mother was Lithuanian. Anyway, Lysander and Maria spoke German together. I could barely understand them. But they fought. You didn't need to know what they were saying."

"It must have been terrible," I said. "The way she died."

"Of course," Bernard said, something cold and fearful creeping into that soft voice. "But before she died, Lysander was moving on. He'd told her that night. She refused a ride home and stomped off. She was always stomping off, but then again Lysander was working, studying. I don't know why they were seeing each other at all, to be honest, but I'm not much for affairs of the heart. She worked as hard as he did, with the piano, the dancing, but every free moment she wanted his attention. He wasn't ready. He was going to go back to Ukraine, to be a scientist, to help his country. She wanted him to stay here."

"So, the woman," Reginald said into the silence that followed, "on the grave, you think...?"

"That it was Maria Zaytseva's ghost," Bernard said flatly. "Of course."

"There," Reginald said to me, an inescapable note of triumph in his voice.

"But where you are mistaken is in the particulars, Mr. Jones," Bernard continued.

Reginald's face screwed up in a question.

"On the night Lysander died," Bernard went on, "He was worse than usual. He wasn't sleeping, eating, nothing. He went to work upstairs in his room. There are only small rooms in this house. I gave him the one with the dormer window. He was tall, and as you can see, I am not.

"There's just a little hallway up there. You can hear everything through the walls. Later that night, very late, I could hear he was talking to someone, but not on the telephone. He was talking as if they were together, in the same room. The pauses, interruptions, I could tell, but I could only hear his half of the conversation. He was talking to someone I could not hear.

"Then, it grew very quiet, and I was worried, so I stepped across and opened the door.

"There Lysander stood, staring out that dormer window, with that gun pointed up at his chin. And outside, floating on the other side of the window, was Maria Zaytseva's ghost, blue and terrible, eyes filled with glee, tears streaking down her cheeks, her mouth a wild grin. Before I could say anything, her hand—her hand passed through that window *and pulled the trigger.*

"No, Mr. Jones, you did not see Maria Zaytseva's ghost crying on the grave of Lysander Kuzma. *She was laughing.*"

About the Author

Jack Opel is a former professor of English and Film Studies, with a PhD in English from UW Madison. Among his other work, he created and taught "Literature and Popular Culture: Horror" for many years. He lives in southern Wisconsin and Baltimore, MD.